NAKODA SUMMER

A story of the

Ya Ha Tinda

By

Cliff Faulknor

Published by
Melanie Faulknor
Edmonton, Alberta
Canada

First published in Canada 2006
by Lulu

ISBN: 978-1-4116-1639-4

DEDICATION

To Corrie my inspiration and my helpmate

INTRODUCTION

It was created and evolved through the mists of early time and evolution was the instrument of its creation. Vast sedimentary basins rose skyward to form the Rocky Mountains – great sheets of ice ground their way southward through the steaming rock. It gouged out deep valleys, carved naked ridges and pulverized solid rock into crude soil. The ice halted and then began a gradual retreat. Rain fell on this new land; the hot sun shone and the surface below sprang into life. Warm winds from the distant seas poured in through the valleys modifying their climates and melting the snows. From the Great Plains to the east came birds bringing their grassland seeds in their dropping, other plant species rode in on air currents on their own. When the grass flourished, the grazing animals came – buffalo, deer, elk, moose and sheep, or primitive versions of them. With the dinner table set, along came the predators – bears, mountain lions, wolves, wolverines, coyotes and weasels. Soaring in on the winds, came the eagles, hawks and owls. Thus was born this mountain eco-system in the Alberta Rockies we call the YA HA TINDA – to the native peoples the "Little Prairie Within the Mountains."

. . . .

ACKNOWLEDGEMENT

A book is the product of many hands, not just the hands of the author. I would like to thank Dr. Bruce Leeson, Dr. Jim Taylor and Dr. Jack Porter of the Western Canada Services Centre, Parks Canada, for providing information on the Ya Ha Tinda, its plant and animal inhabitants and the practices of the peoples who passed through there. This information provided a basis for the book's plot. I would like to thank my doctor, David Sparkes for lending me a book of Nakoda names and Denis Langford, who rode the back trail out of the Ya Ha Tinda as a young man with his father, who was Jasper Park's first Chief Warden. This was the trail Eagle Feather and his people used as an escape route when menaced by a combined force of Blackfoot and Sarcee warriors.

I would also like to thank my friend Corinne Cameron who prodded me out of long writer's block and acted as reader and critic, chapter by chapter, as the book was written.

Cliff Faulknor

CONTENTS

Chapter I

Intruders in the Ya Ha Tinda

It was the first day of the second Moon of the Golden Eagle. Coldmaker's fingers were loosening their grip on the valley as he retreated towards his home in the north. Soon the bright new grass would come and the whole valley would spring into life.

As if to honour this occasion, a great golden eagle left her nest high on a craggy mountain on the western rim. She banked suddenly and the early sun flashed briefly along her golden flanks, then she leveled out and gracefully rode an avenue of wind down over the glistening expanse of Elk River. A moving column of riders going upstream along the gravel bars caught her eye as she swung northwestward and cruised above the yellow grasslands of the intra-mountain valley called the Ya Ha Tinda. She was seeking her morning meal.

Far below her two pairs of dark eyes observed her passage. Two children of the Nakoda tribe - a boy who had seen twelve summers and his sister who had seen fourteen - were riding through the dead grass on an old roan horse. "I am glad I am not a rabbit or a squirrel," Keena said to her brother Wolf Child.

The boy shrugged, "Such creatures are put here by the Great Spirit so they may be eaten. Maybe the sky rider will drop a feather that I can put in my headband like father has."

"Ha," the girl sniffed. "Our father had to fight for his. It did not just drop on his head."

The young Nakodas had not been to the edge of the benchland and therefore had not seen the intruders but their cousin Coyote and older brother Sun Calf had spotted the strange riders right away.

Coyote was the first one to see them as he approached the rim of the upper grasslands. In a flash he had reined in his black mare and slid to the ground before they could see him. He motioned for his cousin Sun Calf to do the same. Quickly they tied their mounts in the shelter of a clump of aspen and then inched their way forward to where they could look down on the river and not be seen from below.

"Sarcee," Coyote muttered. "They should not be here. The Ya Ha Tinda is Nakoda land."

"The Sarcee do not believe that nor do their Blackfoot cousins," Sun Calf said. He had often heard his father Eagle Feather talk about this with the band elders.

"There are eight of them," Coyote counted. "I wonder what they are up to. They do not wear war paint."

"They could be a hunting party," Sun Calf suggested.

"Then why do they not spread out over the valley and hunt?" Coyote wondered.

"At least they are headed up river so they will probably cause us no trouble," his young cousin pointed out. But Sun Calf was worried nonetheless, and his face showed it. Although Sun Calf had seen fourteen winters and considered himself almost a man, he had never seen combat and he wondered how he would stand up to it if came to a fight.

Coyote, who was eighteen, had been on one or two horse raids and enjoyed the excitement. The older youth was tall and strong and much favoured by the girls of their band. Sun Calf idolized him and did not want Coyote to think he was afraid.

"You had better ride back to camp as fast as you can," Coyote said kindly, as he looked down at the anxious face beside him. "Your father must be told about this. We will probably have to get out of here. I will stay and try to find out why they are here, if I could only find a way to get closer to them."

"Be careful cousin," Sun Calf said, as he slid away. "We do not want them to know we are here." Although he knew in his heart, caution was not one of Coyote's attributes.

Sun Calf arrived at the camp just as the two young ones were getting off the roan horse. He was too intent on his mission to return their wave. He went right to his father, Eagle Feather. "There are riders down by the river, father!" he blurted. "We think they are Sarcee. Coyote wants to get closer to them to see if he can find out their purpose."

"He would," Eagle Feather said wryly. Coyote was the son of his brother Deer Stalker. He was a very able youth, quick of action and as powerful as any man in their band, but his nephew was prone to dash into any threatening situation without thinking the thing through. Eagle Feather had had a few misgivings when his brother suggested that he include Coyote in his game scouting party.

"They are not wearing war paint, father," Sun Calf said. "We think they might be a hunting party seeing game in the lower valley. When we saw them, they were headed up river. They may not even come here."

Eagle Feather turned to the old man at his side, who up to this point had remained silent, "What do you make of it father?"

Muskwa shrugged. "I have heard that buffalo are few in number out on the plains. That could be the reason the Sarcee are here, but we have seen no buffalo either. They have forsaken the Ya Ha Tinda because here too the grass is dead." He poked at the sod with a stick he used to aid his walking. "If you put a blanket over the face of a child, the child will die because it will not be able to breathe. The grass must be able to breathe or it too will die. It is the same with all living things. New grass will come slowly because a heavy blanket of old grass is smothering it. If the grass is poor, the buffalo will not come."

Eagle Feather and his family had come here specifically to see if there were buffalo in the valley so they could inform the band. Now it appeared that their journey had been for nothing.

"I think it would be wise for us to leave at once," Eagle Feather said. "If the Sarcee come up here and find us, they will surely take our horses, maybe even kill us when they see that we are few."

He turned to Sun Calf, "You ride out and find Coyote. If he is still where you left him, tell him that both of you are to stay up on the bench. Keep your horses handy and conceal yourselves along the rim. If the Sarcee show any signs of coming up here, get out of there as fast as you can. We will pack up and head north, keeping within the line of trees as much as possible. It will be up to you to find us. You be very careful my son," he added.

Sun Calf swung up onto his pony with a single lithe movement and was soon out of sight.

"I do not like to see our son go out there in the open with the Sarcee so near," said his wife North Star, who had moved up beside them. "He is only a boy. I think we should stay close until he gets back."

"He will be all right. Do not fear," her husband assured her. "He is wise for his years and will not seek trouble."

Night Star was dubious, "He is with Coyote and will try to do anything that Coyote does."

I do not think that Coyote would put him in danger," Eagle Feather said, but in his heart he prayed to the Great Spirit, the High Above One, that his rambunctious nephew would not go down into the river breaks and try to sneak up on the invaders.

The Sarcee were not friendly to the Nakoda. Many, many years ago the Nakoda had come from a land far towards the rising sun and settled along the eastern slopes of the Rocky Mountains. Although the Nakoda outnumbered the Sarcee, the latter were closely allied to the mighty Blackfoot nation which ruled the western plains.

Eagle Feather knew they were too few to fight off an attack by even a small party such as the one the two youths had sighted. They were just five adults and three children, if you counted Coyote as an adult, which you could if it came to a fight. Sun Calf was an unknown quantity. At fourteen he was still very much a boy as his mother said. The two old ones, his father Muskwa and mother Moraha would be of little use in battle. No, the only wise course was to move further up the valley and to rejoin their band as soon as it was safe to take the trail out of the Ya Ha Tinda, Eagle Feather mused.

Down along the rim of the benchland Coyote continued to watch the riders below with interest. They had come to a halt now and were dismounting. They had stopped in a wide, level area where plant growth was heavy, most of it old growth from last year. To his surprise the riders began to slash at the brush with those short axes supplied by the White Traders. His curiosity was aroused. Were they preparing a campsite? If so, this would be bad news for his people. Maybe if he could creep down there through the brush, he could get a better idea of what they were up to. It was a tempting thought.

At that moment, he heard the soft drum of hooves and turned to see Sun Calf leading his horse stealthily forward. Sun Calf tied his mount to a thicket close to where Coyote's black mare was grazing and crept forward on hands and knees. The younger boy was happy to see that Coyote was still where he had left him.

"They are clearing the brush down there, as if for a large campsite," Coyote told him, "if we could only get closer."

Sun Calf shook his head, "My father said we are not to go below the rim and if they show any signs of coming up here, we are to get away as fast as we can. He is breaking camp and moving north up the valley."

Coyote nodded his head. His uncle Eagle Feather was one of Coyote's heroes. Over many campfires the tale has been told how the young Eagle Feather had crouched in a shallow pit all night beside a tethered rabbit waiting for a golden eagle to move in for the kill. Before the big bird could seize its helpless prey Eagle Feather had grabbed the eagle and pulled a large feather from its tail. After a furious struggle and much angry screeching the eagle had torn itself free leaving Coyote's uncle with the prized feather, but bleeding from talon wounds on his neck and face. This is how Eagle Feather had earned his adult name. He could have just downed the eagle with an arrow but this was frowned upon in Nakoda culture. The golden eagle was a sacred symbol. As a boy, Coyote had reveled in this story. He wasn't about to disobey his uncle now.

"Look!" Sun Calf exclaimed. "They are leaving and heading back down river."

Coyote peered over the rim, "Only six of them. Two are still spreading brush around." But the odds were getting much better. Maybe......his thoughts were cut short by the sight of two little columns of smoke beginning to rise from below. "They're setting the brush on fire! Now why would they do that?"

"Maybe this is to be a very big campsite," Sun Calf offered.

"In that case we have to get out of here," Coyote said. "That would mean a lot of Sarcee coming into the Ya Ha Tinda. It is time for us to leave."

It had not taken long for Eagle Feather and his family to pack up and move. All their goods were carried on a single travois. The two older ones rode on one horse, like Keena and Wolf Child. Eagle Feather had his own horse as did his wife, Night Star. Before they left they buried the ashes of their fire and tried to wipe out all tracks. This might be enough to escape the notice of a casual passerby, but would not fool anyone bent on tracking them.

As they rode away, they kept in the shelter of a long finger of spruce and pine, which ran north and south through the grasslands, as Eagle Feather had told Sun Calf they would. When they reached the foot of the mountain range that rimmed the valley to the east they stopped to rest, choosing a spot of high ground which afforded them a clear view over the route they had come. Here they waited for Coyote and Sun Calf to catch up with them, hoping that all had gone well with the boys down below.

Wolf Child was the first to sight them. "There they are!" he cried, as he sighted two riders just emerging from a grove of spruce. They were riding side by side at a leisurely pace as if in no hurry to get there.

Night Star breathed a sigh of relief and grabbed the arm of her husband impulsively.

"They would not be riding like that if they thought there was a danger of pursuit," Eagle Feather smiled. He, too, was relieved to see that the two were safe.

Muskwa and Moraha were a bit more emotional. Of course, it could be that some of the ever-present dust had chosen just that moment to get in their eyes making them water a little. They loved their grandchildren. There was a special bond between Coyote and his grandfather, although he would deny that he favoured any one of them. Coyote, he would often say, was just like he was in his youth, strong and adventurous. He would then go on to relate some of his more daring exploits. If Moraha sniffed occasionally during the telling of these tales, it did not necessarily mean that she disbelieved him; the dry, crisp, mountain air often affected one's nose.

Soon the two riders were among them and there was much smiling and backslapping. Coyote lost no time in telling them what he and Sun Calf had seen down by the river. "They dismounted in a large open area down there and began clearing a lot of the brush," he said, "and then six of them rode off down river leaving two behind. These two then set fire to the piles of brush they had cut. That was when Sun Calf and I decided to get out of there. That fire could spread."

Eagle Feather looked puzzled, "I wonder why they would do that? Do you think that perhaps they were clearing for a new campsite?"

"We thought of that, father," Sun Calf said. "If that is true, it would be a big campsite and that would not be good for our people."

"No it would not," Eagle Feather agreed. "If buffalo are scarce out on the plains, perhaps they mean to move in here and hunt elk and deer."

Old Muskwa added his bit of wisdom. "It is true that large herds of elk winter in the Ya Ha Tinda, but they have gone back into the mountains now. If there are few buffalo on the plains, it means that there, too, the grass is poor. I have been told that long, long ago when the grass did not come, the Great Spirit sent a lance of fire out of the sky setting the old sod on fire until the whole land was aflame. When the fire died, Sun came out and heated the blackened land. The new grass came swiftly after that and with the new grass came the buffalo. When the people of the plains saw this they knew that the Great Spirit was telling them that fire was good for the grass, so in bad grass years they themselves set fire to the lands."

"How do you know this father?" his son queried.

"Our Medicine Man, Otterhead, says that this has been done many times on our plains."

"But here the Sarcee are lighting fires only in the river bottom," Eagle Feather reminded him. "Coyote and Sun Calf saw them set their fires and leave."

"We did not see the last two leave uncle," Coyote said. "They were still lighting fires when we left. We were afraid the fires might spread."

Eagle Feather was not convinced. He still favoured the idea that the Sarcee planned to make a big camp in the Ya Ha

Tinda. However, he made a mental note to bring this matter of improving grassland by burning to the attention of the Band Council when they got back to the main camp at Clear Water, if they would still listen that is. He had been completely at outs with them when he and his family left.

The Nakoda were more fortunate than the plains people as far as food supply was concerned because they lived in the mountains where elk, moose and deer were plentiful. They did not have to rely so heavily on the buffalo for food, clothing and shelter. Nakoda lodges were often sheathed with tree bark. It made sense that the Sarcee and others would come into the mountains in a year when buffalo were scarce.

But all this could be determined later. Right now Eagle Feather had to get his family safely back to Clear Water. Game had been so scarce they were running short of food. He decided that the quickest way home was to travel south again, keeping within the cover of the hills until they reached the pass which led over the mountains. This would bring them close to the river again, but they would be traveling some distance above the grasslands, so there was little chance they would be detected. Quickly he outlined his plan to the others.

"We must move quickly," he said. "There is too much danger for us here."

Coyote did not know whether to side with his grandfather or his uncle in their theories as to why the Sarcee were here. They were here and must be avoided at this time. Later perhaps there would be a day of reckoning.

They had traveled only a short distance when the air became pungent. It stung their nostrils.

"I smell smoke," Sun Calf cried.

"I smell it too," his father nodded gravely. "Could it be that the Sarcee have come up the valley and made camp somewhere near us? Coyote you ride higher up on the slope. Perhaps you will be able to locate it."

"Smoke hurts noses," Wolf Child complained.

Coyote had ridden only a little way up when he came racing back at a gallop. "The whole lower end of the Ya Ha Tinda is on fire!"

"The Sarcee fires must have spread," old Muskwa nodded. "I knew that something would go wrong. It generally does. If the wind should rise, we are finished." As if to give force to his words, the wind did begin to increase in intensity.

Eagle Feather was annoyed with his father. "We will be quite safe if we stay up on the mountain," he snapped, afraid the old man's words might unduly alarm the others. "The fire will not climb into the pass because there is still snow under the trees," but he was worried nonetheless.

They had reached higher ground now which gave them a clear view of the clouds of billowing smoke to the south.

"Look at all the birds," Keena cried, pointing down near the edge of the smoke where eagles and hawks were wheeling and diving.

Grandmother Moraha nodded. "The burrowers are fleeing the fire and the killers are having a fine feast."

Some distance ahead of them three deer appeared on the run as they, too, fled the smoke. They were headed for the safety of the deep forest above.

"We are short of food uncle," Coyote said. "Maybe Sun Calf and I should ride after them and kill one."

"We do not have the time," Eagle Feather said regretfully. "Soon they will be up into heavy growth where the cover is too dense for you to follow them."

Watching the rapid pace of the advancing fire as it raced up the slope, he suddenly realized they would soon be in a race for their lives. Should they dismount and turn their horses loose, abandon their belongings and try to follow the deer to safety? No, their progress would be too slow because of the snow cover higher up and the smoke might get to them.

"It would be better for us to stay on horseback," said Night Star, as if reading his thoughts.

He nodded agreement. "Come!" he shouted. "We must move faster."

****

Chapter II

Trapped

They had come to a place where the pine and spruce trees were thin and there was a fairly heavy undercover of grass. Away below them gleamed the waters of a lake. They knew they were not far from the pass now, but a glance ahead told Eagle Feather and the others that they would never be able to reach it. A heavy pall of thick smoke was beginning to roll through the trees, stinging their nostrils and causing their eyes to water.

"We must head for the lake," shouted Eagle Feather. Already they could hear the roar and crackle of the flames. Soon it would be among them, devouring the grass greedily as it came. If it got up into the trees, they would find themselves dodging burning brands of fire as branches fell among them.

"We will never make it," Muskwa said gloomily. "The way down is too steep and rough."

"Be quiet old man," his wife Moraha scolded. "You will alarm the children."

"I am not afraid to die," Sun Calf told her, which was his way of saying that he resented being classed as a child. Riding beside him, Coyote touched his arm reassuringly.

"Be quiet everyone and tend to your horses," Eagle Feather snapped. "They will need guidance. We are not going to die. Fire does not often burn downhill. Waves of rising heat carry it upward."

"Waves of heat also eat up the air, so it will be hard for us to breathe," Muskwa grunted. Then an angry look from his wife told him it would be a good time to be silent. They made their way safely to the water's edge, but not without a few scary moments. At one time it seemed that the travois would push ahead of the old roan pulling it. Down, down they plunged, slipping and sliding at every step. Once the horse carrying Muskwa and Moraha stumbled and almost threw them, as the old man predicted that it would. Coyote was beside them in a moment grabbing the horse's bridle.

Behind and above them raged the fire. The spot on the hill where they had paused was now aflame, but the rising heat did keep the smoke above them and there was still enough air for them to breathe.

Across the water they could see a steep wall of sheer rock rising almost from the edge of the lake. To the left of it though, they saw a pebble beach and the beach was located on the far side of the rock wall, well away from the path of the fire. By now the searing heat was becoming stifling for both people and horses.

"Into the water!" Eagle Feather shouted. "We will swim across. The travois will float. If the horses begin to falter get off them and cling to their saddles. It is not far. Sun Calf you look after the young ones."

Wolf Child did not like the idea of his brother having to look after them. He and Keena knew how to swim a horse.

The sharp bite of the mountain water was a bit of a shock to them at first, but it soon proved to be a welcome relief from the heat of the fire: even the horses seemed to enjoy it.

They arrived on the other side without any trouble and climbed gratefully onto the rocky shore. Their sleeping robes and other possessions were undamaged, wrapped tightly in elk skins. The air was much purer here. They gazed back in awe at the raging inferno across the water and marveled at their escape. As they watched, a large white-tailed buck plunged into the lake, its back afire. It began to climb weakly out of the water near them. Its hide was still smoking. Raising his bow carefully, Sun Calf took aim and sent an arrow into its chest. The deer collapsed dead on the beach. Coyote applauded him for his quick action.

Keena cried out in protest, "It was only seeking safety as we ourselves did. You are no better than the hawks and eagles."

"It would not have lived anyway," Coyote assured her. "And we have to have food for our journey."

"All we have left is a small bit of berry pemmican," Night Star told her daughter. "As Coyote, said we are in need of food. We will say a prayer to the spirit of the deer and thank it for providing us with meat," her mother assured her.

Eagle Feather took a knife from his belt and began to skin the animal carefully. There was no time to let the meat hang for awhile. The women needed it now so they could make their dinner. The pemmican would be saved for when they were traveling.

The sun had already reached the rim of the western mountains and the sky was darkening. Sun Calf and Wolf Child were sent to look for wood on the fireside of the sheltering rock to fuel their cooking fire. Coyote went along to help them. Some of the partly burned tree branches they brought back were still glowing. Soon they had a good campfire on the go.

Night Star and Keena climbed up among the rock outcrops in search of wild carrots and other edible roots. Down on the beach Moraha was already preparing the fresh meat for cooking. When that was done, she then dug a hole in the rocky ground about the size of a small bucket. This she lined with wet rawhide and then half filled with water. Under her instructions, the two boys had collected some smooth stones from around the lake and were heating them in the fire. Next, Moraha put the meat and roots into the hole.

"Now bring me those hot stones," she commanded.

"They're too hot to touch," Wolf Child complained. "I'll burn my hands," but he was just complaining to make himself heard. He knew how to get a stick and push the hot stone onto a picce of tree branch. "Come, I'll help you," Coyote laughed.

One by one the hot stones were dropped into the mixture of deer meat and roots.

Then everyone just stood around watching Moraha stir the stew. "Now that the White Man has built a trading post on

River Boiling, we may soon be able to get some of those metal pots I hear people talking about, mother," Eagle Feather remarked. "It will then be easier for you to prepare a meal."

"The White Man has his ways and we have ours," she sniffed.

Old Muskwa chuckled, "Because we cook this way, the White Man calls us the Stoneys."

"The Whites appear to want to put their own names on everything and everybody," Night Star observed.

Darkness had now fallen and with it the raging fires above had abated. The angry roar of the flames had become a mutter, with the occasional popping sound or flare up as the heat ignited a pocket of pitch. With the fading of the light, the trees no longer provided oxygen for the flames to feed on. After their meal was finished, the family built up the fire and then gathered around to meditate or chat as the spirit moved them, as people have done since the dawn of history. With the firelight playing on their faces, each became absorbed in his or her own thoughts. Except the young ones, for them this was a time for story telling.

"Grandfather," Wolf Child said, breaking the silence. "Tell us about the Nakoda and how we came to be in this place."

"This I have told you often," Muskwa grunted, but he was not displeased that he had been asked. All he needed was a bit of coaxing.

"Tell us again, grandfather," Keena urged.

"Yes, tell us again," Night Star nodded, although she knew from experience that nothing could have stopped him now.

Muskwa cleared his throat, as if to get everyone's attention. "Many, many years ago our people lived far away from here towards the rising sun," he began. "We were a part of one of the proudest warrior nations of them all, the Lakota Sioux. Our neighbors called us the Parted Hairs and they feared us greatly. Then the White Man came to our land and brought us a terrible sickness. They called it the smallpox. Some of our tribes lost more than half their people. While we were still free of this disease, we fled north to escape it – north to the land of Coldmaker. The people of the north were called the Cree, as you know. They were not hostile to us at that time and allowed us to settle among them. We became known as the Assiniboine."

Sun Calf asked, "And how did we get away out here in the Backbone?"

"Some of our people began to hear tales around the campfires about the great mountains that lay far toward the setting sun. They were called the Backbone because they divided the flowing waters of this great island on which we live. Game was plentiful in this land we were told, so about three bands set out to find it. The Cree told these people to keep well to the north as they journeyed, for the western plains were the home of the mighty Blackfoot nation, who would kill us if we intruded upon their land. In time these ancestors of ours did reach the great mountains, where they made a place for themselves within the shelter of the hills."

"Do you think it was good that we came to this place, grandfather?" Keena asked.

Muskwa shrugged. "The Great Spirit must have willed it, for we have done well here."

Eagle Feather got up and stretched his legs. "It is time we went to our sleeping robes," he smiled. "Perhaps if we rise early we will get through the pass while the fire demons are still sleeping." Coyote was already rolled up in his sleeping robe.

And so, it proved to be. It was still dark when the family moved out from their encampment and climbed into the open park-like heights above the lake. The grass here under the trees had burned quickly, then died out for lack of fuel. Most of the big trees were only blackened around their bases. The travelers soon encountered snow, which deepened as the trail climbed.

Everyone heaved a sigh of relief; they were safe now. By daybreak they had reached the pass which would lead them out of the mountains. Looking down on the blackened grasslands of the Ya Ha Tinda, Night Star shivered. "It all seems so dead down there, everywhere you look you see only blackness."

"After death comes the new life," her father-in-law consoled her. "That is the way the Great Spirit has ordered it."

They stopped to rest in a small meadow near the source of a little river on the other side of the pass. Because they had left the lake so early, it was felt that the old ones would need to rest awhile. The horses were tired too and needed to feed for awhile on the old grass that lay knee deep around them. "We are in no great hurry to get to Clear Water. We are safe now," Eagle Feather said. "One more sleep should see us there."

"I would like to get back as soon as we can," Night Star told him. Moraha nodded in agreement. They had many friends and relatives in the band and were anxious to see them. Most

Nakoda bands were made up of blood relatives or relatives by marriage. It was like one big extended family.

Muskwa glanced at his son resignedly. Neither of them was that anxious to get back. It would mean they would both have to eat humble pie. Long had they boasted that they would bring back buffalo meat and hides. Now they would have to admit they had found no buffalo in the Ya Ha Tinda.

In the first moon of the Golden Eagle, Chief Many Elk had convinced their band council that all but the most infirm should move to a spring hunting camp as soon as possible. It had been a mild winter along River Boiling, the great stream that ran past their winter camp. The trail south was mostly clear, he had heard. The Chief had itchy feet. He believed that if you stayed too long in one place, problems were sure to develop. Because he was Chief, problems always landed at his feet. Better to keep everybody on the move. People had no time to squabble when they were busy traveling or setting up new camps.

That was how the band came to be at Clear Water. When they had arrived at the great wide flats by the river, the Chief had persuaded the council that here was the place to stop. Game was plentiful, the river was full of fish and in the Moon of Red Berries the bushes around them would be full of fruit.

Eagle Feather had hotly disagreed with this decision. "What we need is a place where there are buffalo," he said. "There have been no buffalo at Clear Water for many years. Buffalo provide more meat and have bigger and stronger hides. Our long ago ancestors were hunters of buffalo. I hear there are buffalo in the Ya Ha Tinda."

"We are Nakoda. We do not have to depend on buffalo," the Chief pointed out. "Leave the buffalo to the Blackfoot and the Sarcee. They have many swift horses. We do not."

The Council agreed with the Chief. Hunting the buffalo could put them in conflict with their enemies. Many were becoming weary of the trail.

"The Ya Ha Tinda is Nakoda land," Eagle Feather had argued, but to no avail. Angrily he had stormed out of the meeting. Old Muskwa had followed him. The two of them had decided they would pull out of the band and take their families to the Ya Ha Tinda. Eagle Feather's two brothers had decided to stay with the band. Coyote had begged his uncle to take him along.   He knew if he stayed in camp, he would be given onerous chores that a warrior should not be asked to do.

When the time came for Eagle Feather and Muskwa and their families to leave, nobody paid much attention to them. Everyone was busy building new shelters.   Nakoda families often went off by themselves for some reason or another. It was a free and open society.

Now Eagle Feather and Muskwa would have to face the jeers of their people.   Brother Black Wolf would say, "I can already taste the buffalo hump you are going to give me," or brother Deer Stalker would say, "Next winter we will enjoy those buffalo robes you have for us."

****

Chapter III

The Home Coming

Coyote was of two minds about getting back to the band. Setting up a big new campsite meant a lot of tedious work that had to be done. This is something he always tried to avoid if possible. He considered physical labour to be undignified for a person of his caliber. Then there was his cousin, Crocus, daughter of Black Wolf, his father's younger brother. She was a pest, always trailing along asking questions, hanging on his every word. One thing for sure, she would be waiting in the welcoming crowd he knew would gather the moment his party was sighted.

"There's our camp," Wolf Child shouted excitedly, as the family reached the south bank of the river. "Look at all the lodges."

It was true the camp had grown in their absence. It was a sea of new teepees, some made of tree bark and some just made of poles with chinks filled with moss or dried mud. The place had the settled look of a major encampment.

Their arrival was announced by the excited barking of the camp dogs. One in particular rushed joyfully to meet them. This was Kakwa, Eagle Feather's own dog that he had regretfully had to leave behind because the animal had a sore paw. Crowds of people soon appeared. This time their return caused a lot of excitement. Some Nakodas from the Cold Water band far to the south had ridden up a few days ago to report that there was much smoke in the Ya Ha Tinda. Close friends and relatives of the Eagle Feather family had been very concerned for their safety.

As the crowd swarmed around them at the outskirts of the big camp, Coyote noticed with some surprise that Crocus was not among them. This was odd. She was usually one of the first to greet him. Not that her absence mattered, of course. On the contrary he was relieved she was not there he told himself. It was just that, well, he was accustomed to seeing her face whenever he rode in.

As expected, brothers Deer Stalker and Black Wolf had a little fun at their older brother's expense when they saw the almost empty travois.

"Is not your mouth watering for taste of buffalo hump brother?" Black Wolf said to Deer Stalker.

"It is," Deer Stalker nodded, smacking his lips noisily.

Eagle Feather took their joshing good-naturedly. "As you can see, we have none," he smiled. "The grass was old and matted there, but I am told that the fire will end that." Then he gave them an account of the fire's fury and how they had barely gotten away with their lives. They all sobered up after that and wanted to know all the details of their escape.

"I see many lodges," Eagle Feather said. "I will have to get busy and build one." He was beginning to feel that he had acted very rashly charging off like that when the camp was just getting started. Others had been left to do the work.

"You will not want for shelter, brother," Black Wolf told him affectionately. "There is plenty of room in our lodges." He was just relieved that everyone was back safely.

"We have no food either," Moraha told her youngest son.

Black Wolf laughed, "You think I would let you starve, mother? Since when did we not share with one other? There is plenty of food. The hunt has been good here. We have shot many elk and deer."

"I hope they were bucks," his father Muskwa said. "You must not shoot mothers when they are raising their young."

"Only bucks, father," his son assured him.

"I shot a deer when we were running from the fire," Sun Calf told them, but nobody seemed to be paying much attention to him except Coyote. "If you had not, cousin, we would have gone hungry," Coyote assured him.

Wolf Child and Keena had already run off with the other band children. Sun Calf decided he might as well join them for all the notice he got around here.

It was decided that Eagle Feather and his family would stay with Deer Stalker and that Muskwa and Moraha would stay with their youngest son, Black Wolf and his wife Grey Dawn. For one thing, Moraha and Deer Stalker's wife Morning Cloud did not get along too well. Some years ago Morning Cloud had given birth to a baby that died soon after delivery and she blamed her mother-in-law Moraha for it. Moraha had been acting as midwife.

Darkness fell quickly as soon as the sun disappeared behind the western mountains. Away off somewhere on the river's south shore, a wolf began to howl and was soon joined by others of his pack. Several of the camp dogs decided to join the chorus too. Although Coldmaker had departed, the night was still a bit chilly because of the elevation. Bright fires were glowing in all the lodges, which gave a ghost-like appearance to the whole encampment. On such a night it was good to gather around a glowing fire to talk and recall the events of the day. The three families had gathered in Black Wolf's lodge because he, too, had been away and had much to tell them. While Eagle Feather and his family had been in the Ya Ha Tinda, Black Wolf had taken the winter's furs that he and his brothers had collected and gone to the trading post the White Man had built on River Boiling. The Nakodas called the big log structures Old House, although its builders had named it Rocky Mountain House.

While they sat and talked, the firelight played softly on their faces. Outside dogs snarled and fought over the scraps of elk meat that had been tossed to them after the evening meal.

Black Wolf laid out several brightly colored woolen blankets for them to see. Everyone had to feel these items and most agreed that they were softer and felt warmer to the touch than their deerskin clothing. The exception was old Moraha, of course.

"They feel good because they are new," she sniffed. "But how will they feel after a few washings in the river?"

"Well, mother," Black Wolf laughed, "here is something that you might find useful," and took out several large and small pots and kettles made of iron. "You can put these in the hottest fire and they will not burn," he told them.

Night Star, Grey Dawn, and Morning Cloud were very interested in these but Moraha picked one of them up and then dropped it again as if it had been in the fire. "They are too heavy," she said.

Then Black Wolf went to the back of the lodge and brought out his proudest possession. It was one of the White Man's 'fire sticks', an old flintlock muzzleloader that had seen better days, but to Black Wolf it meant power and prestige in the band, not to mention within his family. He had always felt a little inferior because he was shorter than the other two. He also brought out a powder horn and some lead bullets.

Deer Stalker and Eagle Feather exchanged glances. If their younger brother had a gun, as the White Man called it, and learned how to use it effectively, he might become the number one hunter in the band and outshine the both of them. This brought up the question of how many furs did Black Wolf have to pay for this gun? Did some of the furs they had collected go to pay for this new weapon?

As if reading their thoughts, Black Wolf said quickly, "This gun belongs to our family, of course. We will all share it. While I was in the store of the trader, the Great Spirit spoke to me and urged me to buy it, saying to me that this would be a good thing for our family and the band."

This made the two older brothers feel a bit better about the gun. It was to be family property.

Eagle Feather got up and stretched. "Daylight will come early," he said, "and there is much work to do."

Deer Stalker rose too, as did Coyote. Night Star and Morning Cloud had been ready to leave for some time, but they had decided to let the men talk themselves out. Looking around for the children they found them to be sound asleep, along with Black Wolf's two, Crocus and the baby, Badger. They decided to just leave them there.

Morning dawned bright and clear, except for a thin mist, which hovered over the river. Outside of Deer Stalker's lodge, a bunch of magpies were picking away at the bones left by the dogs the night before. The big hound, Kakwa, raised his head and looked at the magpies for a moment then went back to sleep again. He did not feel like chasing magpies this morning. When he did he always seemed to come off second best.

The flap of Black Wolf's teepee opened and out came Sun Calf, Wolf Child and Keena. They had already eaten because their grandmother, Moraha, was not one to remain in her sleeping robe when the sun was up. Now the young ones were wondering what they could do to put in the day. They did not have to wonder very long. Eagle Feather came around from behind the lodge with one of the new hatchets that Black Wolf had brought from Old House.

"Just what I'm looking for," he grinned. "Some willing workers to help me gather spruce bark and poles so I can build a lodge."

Work was not what the three of them had in mind, but they did not have much choice here. Ingrained in them almost from birth was obedience to one's elders. When Coyote joined them they felt much better about it. All three admired their older cousin. For his part, Coyote was not very happy about this turn of events either.

All morning they laboured, bringing in the bark that Eagle feather had peeled from around the base of each tree. Because it was springtime and the sap was running strongly, the tree did not receive permanent damage. Eagle Feather had to admit that the metal axe had made the task much easier.

His next job was to cut a bunch of thin poles from a stand of lodgepole pine. These too were hauled into camp. By this time the young ones had made a game of it and laughed and shouted while they worked. In the meantime, Crocus had come out to join them, spending most of her time helping Coyote. Coyote could not understand a feeling that suddenly came over him. Crocus had changed in some mysterious way. What had happened to the gawky girl he had grown up with? More puzzling still, he was actually happy that she was there.

A building site was chosen close to the lodges of Deer Stalker and Black Wolf. The poles were arranged in teepee shape then covered with the spruce bark. Where cracks were found these were sealed with mud, from the riverbanks. As this was not a winter camp, no second wall was needed.

As they were putting finished touches to the new lodge, Chief Many Elk came up with three band elders. Eagle Feather greeted them a bit sheepishly. The last time he had seen these elders was at the meeting where he had stormed out of the big lodge in a fit of anger because they had all voted to make their summer camp here at Clear Water.

After the usual polite greetings the Chief got down to business. "The Council will meet tonight in the big lodge," he said. "We want to hear more about your adventures in the Ya Ha Tinda."

Eagle Feather decided he had better make a clean breast of it. It was time to eat his humble pie. "There is not much to tell. We did not stay very long. There were no buffalo and no buffalo signs. It was a mistake to go there."

"That does not matter now," the Chief waved his hand airily. "Many of the things you said at that meeting made sense. These flats here where we have made our camp will never attract buffalo. There is a lot of brush here, but no large areas of good grass. Brush and shrubs may be good for deer and elk, but not for buffalo. It would be good for the band to have a buffalo hunt."

With that the Chief made off with his companions to tell others about the meeting tonight. While this talk had been going on the youngsters had listened with awe. It seemed that big things were afoot. Maybe they would be allowed to attend. At least Coyote would get to go and he could tell them about it later.

A call from their grandfather informed them that a meal was ready. Because the day was warm and clear, a fire had been built outside of their lodge. They suddenly realized how hungry they were. Their grandmother, Moraha, had prepared the meal for all three families. Black Wolf had supplied a loin of elk meat for the occasion and had talked his mother into trying out one of the new metal pots. She and her daughters-in-law and Keena had been out on the flats all morning, gathering wild carrots and other roots to add to the boiling meat.

"You see, mother, how much easier it is to cook this way," Morning Cloud had said. "No hole to dig, no hot rocks."

But old Moraha was not admitting to anything, especially to Morning Cloud. She just sniffed disdainfully and looked out across the flats as if she had seen something of interest there.

It had been decided that they would all eat together because Eagle Feather had not had a chance to go hunting. Black Wolf had a good supply of venison and elk meat. Deer Stalker had shot a moose. If the whole band had been hungry, it would have been the same. The brothers would have shared with them.

After the meal was over Eagle Feather and his two brothers went off up river to look for game, while the three younger women leveled the floor of the new lodge and lined it with grass, Moraha sat around and watched them. She had prepared the meal and now it was time for her to rest. There was much talk among them about the meeting to be held that night. Muskwa came in and joined the conversation. All agreed that they would be there to see what the Council had in mind.

Just about everyone in the band had made the same decision. There were so many that most had to sit outside. A big fire was lit in front of the Council lodge and certain band members who got inside volunteered to relay what was said there to those outside.

The Council lodge was a much larger structure than the usual family teepee. As the band planned to stay in this location for the summer and fall, the Council had decided to build a lodge similar to the one at their winter encampment on River Boiling. It was a pole and moss building about fourteen feet high, twelve feet wide, and some twenty feet long by the White

Man's measure. In fact, it was quite similar to some of the buildings around the Old House trading post. To straighten the structure, a double layer of poles and moss formed the walls. The fire was located at one end, not in the centre as in circular teepees.

Some had suggested that the meeting itself should be held outside, but the Councilmen objected, especially the older ones who were somewhat stiff of limb. Nights in the foothill country were still cold at this time of year.

The Council lodge belonged to no one. It was communal property, which could be used to house visitors from other bands when not being used for meetings.

After a few formalities had been completed, Eagle Feather was invited to tell everybody about his trip to Elk River and the Ya Ha Tinda. Word had gotten around about the Sarcee coming in and setting fire to the grasslands in the hope of attracting the buffalo. Everyone craned forward to listen.

The Chief was very interested in this. "Why would one destroy the grass to make the buffalo come when the buffalo will not come unless there is grass?" he wondered.

One of the band's best hunters, Moosekiller, rose to tell what he had heard on a trip he had taken to visit his wife's people, the Northern Cree. "It was told around the campfires that when you burned old grass the new growth coming up beneath it could breathe better and therefore would grow faster and stronger," he said. "It is known that where there is good grass the buffalo will come in great numbers."

"I have heard this too," old Muskwa told the assembly.

Many Elk thought about this a moment then he nodded, "This makes good sense. If the buffalo come into the Ya Ha Tinda, they are on our land and we can hunt them. If we hunt them on the plains, we face attack from the Sarcee and the Blackfoot."

"If the Sarcee set fire to the grass in the Ya Ha Tinda, it means they intend to hunt there," one of the elders pointed out.

"This is true," Moosekiller agreed, "but we have more people than the Sarcee, we are stronger. It is only the Blackfoot that we would have to fear. It has been said that they do not hunt above Elk River."

"But the Ya Ha Tinda is on Elk River," another elder said, "or only a short way above it."

"I have been to the Ya Ha Tinda," a man named Yellow Bird nodded, "and what he says is true."

"We need buffalo," Moosekiller said stubbornly. "Their hides are bigger and thicker and will keep us warmer when Coldmaker comes and buffalo meat would be a welcome change for us."

"If the buffalo come to the Ya Ha Tinda, they are our buffalo," most of the Council finally agreed.

Chief Many Elk figured it was time for him to make a decision, "The Sarcee would probably not send a big party into the Ya Ha Tinda to hunt until the Moose Breeding Moon," he said. "What we need is someone to go in there during the Grass Moon to tell us if the new grass has indeed come and to let us know if the buffalo come in to eat it."

Eagle Feather rose, a bit sheepishly and volunteered to go back to the Ya Ha Tinda with his family and camp there so he could report if the buffalo came. He felt that he needed to redeem his reputation after promising everybody fresh buffalo meat the last time. His brother, Deer Stalker, jumped up and said he would go with him. Black Wolf got up to say that he should be the one to go with Eagle Feather because he had a gun, but on second thought decided this was a family matter and sat down again.

"Hoy, hoy," the crowd shouted, "send Deer Stalker and Eagle Feather!"

As this appeared to be the will of the people, the Council quickly agreed that this was the thing to do.

"When we hear that the buffalo are there, we will bring most of our best hunters in and set up a hunting camp," the Chief pronounced.

The Council lingered for awhile smoking their pipes, and convincing themselves that they had made the right decision. This being also a social occasion, nobody seemed in a hurry to go home. Word of the decision was passed on to those outside and the whole business was thrashed out again. The talk went on for the rest of the evening.

When Coyote heard the news, he could have jumped for joy. Soon he would be on the move again. Like Chief Many Elk he preferred movement to labour. This time it would be a different story if they encountered a Sarcee patrol!

****

Chapter IV

The Moon of New Grass

The deep rich green of spring ran through the willows that lay along the banks of Clear Water. Nesting birds were busy tending their young. Often they burst into song. It was a time of renewal. The river itself was fairly quiet: awaiting the rampaging flood stage when building heat in the mountains would start to melt the snow.

"It is time for us to go," Eagle Feather told his brother Deer Stalker one morning, "while the river is still low enough for us to cross."

Deer Stalker agreed. While they were talking, Black Wolf came up and once more put forth his case that he was the logical one to go with his brother, Eagle Feather, because he had the gun. Because he was younger and shorter than the other two, he felt that they did not take him seriously. He had thought that owning the gun would change that.

"I seem to remember you saying something about this being a family gun," Deer Stalker said with a wink at Eagle Feather. "Perhaps we should take it with us."

"You would not know how to use it," Black Wolf retorted. "It takes much practice and I have had that practice."

The others laughed. "The last time I saw you fire it, it knocked you flat on the ground."

"I had put in too much powder," Black Wolf said sheepishly, "but I know the right amount now."

"When you come in later with the hunting party you will be well skilled in the use of it," Eagle Feather said diplomatically. "In the meantime there is the question of the old ones. They will be happier here with you and Grey Dawn."

Black Wolf saw his point. If his mother had to live with Morning Cloud, there would not be much harmony in his brother's lodge. He finally agreed that Deer Stalker was the one to go. They decided that the younger children should also stay with Black Wolf. Keena would be a companion for her cousin, Crocus, and the two girls could help to care for the old ones, Muskwa and Moraha.

When Keena heard of this she was quite happy with the arrangement, but Crocus, who had seventeen winters, would have preferred to go with the advance party, mainly because Coyote would be there. Changes had been taking place in her over the past winter. She no longer saw Coyote as the good-natured companion of her childhood. She took note of how tall he had grown: his broad shoulders and the natural grace of his movements. Coyote would be a great hunter someday, she told herself.

The biggest problem for the band in planning a major buffalo hunt was the availability of suitable horses. The Nakoda had not been using horses for very long. Not too many years ago their travois had been pulled by dogs. They were not rich in horses and the ones they had were not up to the quality of the horses owned by the plain's tribes. That was one more good reason for them to do their hunting within the confines of the Ya Ha Tinda. The Nakoda were not equipped to seek buffalo on the open plains. Not to mention the danger of attack from the Blackfoot and Sarcee.

Eagle Feather and Deer Stalker knew of these dangers, which is why they had decided to leave the young ones at Clear Water. But when Wolf Child was told that he was to be left behind with his sister, he raised such a fuss that they finally relented and told him that he could go.

"We could use him to look after the horses," Deer Stalker said.

"And I will need someone to collect wood for our fires," his mother Night Star added. She knew that her youngest would be heartbroken if left behind.

They pulled out at dawn the following day, and this time most of the camp was there to see them off. There were eight of them all told, and all their supplies were carried on two travois. These included elk skin teepees, which were light and easily put up. There were also deerskin sleeping robes, two of the cooking pots that Black Wolf had traded for at Old House, two of the new metal axes and some extra moccasins and clothing. For food they had a quantity of berry pemmican, but this would not last them very long. Most of their food would have to come from the game they found in the Ya Ha Tinda. The men were armed with their lances, bows and arrows, and each had a knife stuck in his belt.

As they got ready to cross the river, their Medicine Man, Otterhead, approached Eagle Feather and Deer Stalker. "I have asked the Great Spirit to guard you on your journey," he said. "But still a prudent man will always take measures to assist the

Great Spirit in his task. If the Sarcee should come again, they will come in by Elk River and occupy the south end of the valley. If you were camped there, you might not be able to escape over the pass. It is too near the river. Do you follow me?"

Both Eagle Feather and Deer Stalker nodded agreement.

"Then it would be wise to camp near the far end where the valley is very narrow. An old trail leads north from there along a creek, which flows in the Ya Ha Tinda. This trail will bring you all the way to Clear Water. It may take longer to reach here by that trail, but you will be safer. The Sarcee will not follow you into those narrow canyons."

"Remember, if you see buffalo, send word back to us at once," Chief Many Elk said. The Chief fully intended to accompany the hunting party himself. He was not young, but his feet were itching to be on the road again. Otterhead could look after the Clear Water camp in his absence. If Otterhead's medicine was as powerful as he claimed, running the camp should be easy for him.

Crossing the river did not present any problem. Eagle Feather rode in the lead, followed by Deer Stalker, Coyote and

Sun Calf. Wolf Child, much to his disgust, rode behind his mother on the old roan horse that pulled their travois. Behind them came Morning Cloud with her travois. Bounding along happily beside them was their big hound Kakwa. Eagle Feather figured they had better take the dog on this trip. They might need Kakwa's keen sense of smell and hearing to warn them of approaching danger.

In the excitement of their departure, nobody noticed the lone rider on a height of land downstream from the Nakoda encampment. From her vantage point, Crocus could see the scouting party long after they had passed from the view of the people below. When she, too, could no longer see the travelers, she rode slowly down to join the others.

The sun had just begun to appear above the eastern horizon. All signs told them it would be a clear, warm spring day.

"Unless we run into trouble, we should reach the pass into the Ya Ha Tinda well before dark," Eagle Feather said to his brother, who had pulled up beside him.

"There should be no trouble with the Sarcee or Blackfoot, as long as we keep within the hills," the other said.

In late afternoon they reached the small river that had its source high up near the pass. When they came to the little meadow where Eagle Feather and his family had stopped on their way home during the first Moon of the Golden Eagle they stopped to rest their horses and themselves. The Ya Ha Tinda lay just a short distance beyond the pass. With their goal almost within sight, they did not linger long in the meadow.

Their next stop was at a clearing that commanded a view of the whole valley below.

And what a beautiful scene greeted their eyes! The whole of the Ya Ha Tinda was covered in a mantle of fresh green growth from the low lying lands along the river to the upper benchland, which stretched away to the north.

"How beautiful it is!" Night Star cried. It was she who had been so saddened by all the blackness left by the raging fire.

Farther down they did run into signs of the fire. Most of the tree trunks were blackened around the base, but the grass and shrubs of the undergrowth had recovered surprisingly well, even though they were unable to receive the full warmth of the sun because of their location.

Below them the lake glistened invitingly. "Maybe we should make our camp down there," Deer Stalker suggested. "Tomorrow we will have plenty of time to look for a permanent campsite."

Eagle Feather shook his head. "We would be in a deep hole down there where others could see us, but we would not be able to see them. It was a good place to seek refuge from the fire, but a poor place to be caught by an enemy hunting party. We would be wiser to go to the edge of the trees and check for any movement down in the meadows before we go any further."

As far as they could see, there was none. The Ya Ha Tinda appeared to be clear of man or beast. Even that did not completely reassure Eagle Feather. The trouble that they had on their first trip had made him very wary. Who knows what may lie in those bands of trees, which bisected the grasslands? By now the sun was nearing the rim of the western mountains.

"We will camp here," he decided. "If anyone is camped down there, we will be able to see the glow of their campfires."

They made a small cooking fire down in a hollow where it could not be seen from below and prepared their evening meal. There was a depression nearby that was filled with water from the melting snow where their horses could drink. Wolf Child gathered some of the fire debris to feed their little cooking fire. Grazing was scanty, but there were small pockets of old grasses that had not been burned.

Darkness fell quickly as the sun disappeared. Then they saw it, the faint glow of a campfire down there among the trees.

"We were wise not to go down there, brother," Deer Stalker said. "I wonder who they are? At least there appears to be only one fire."

"And it is only a small fire," Coyote added.

Eagle Feather nodded, "But we have to know who they are and how many are down there."

"I will creep down and try to find out," Sun Calf offered.

"No, you will not," his mother said sharply. "You could get yourself killed, even if they are not enemies. If someone spotted your movements, they might think you were an enemy and kill you."

"Your mother is right," Eagle Feather said. "We must wait until it is almost dawn. They will be sleeping soundly then and will be slow to react to any intruders. First we will have to scout around and find how many horses they have. That will give us a clue to their strength."

They had ridden far that day, but still sleep did not come easily to them. They had not expected to find any human presence in the Ya Ha Tinda, especially when there did not seem to be any buffalo. This could put a crimp in their plans for a big hunt. Only Wolf Child appeared to be sleeping soundly, with his head resting on the back of their dog Kakwa. And that was another thing which puzzled Eagle Feather, the dog did not seem to sense that there was danger near. Even though the strange camp was some distance away, Kakwa's ears would have detected the sounds of people and horses.

Eagle Feather and Deer Stalker came awake just as the first traces of light began to filter into the eastern sky through the trees behind them. As the two older men were stretching their limbs and wondering how to proceed, Coyote awoke and looked at them with an unspoken question in his eyes. Everyone was beginning to stir now, except for Wolf Child and the dog.

"We must move quickly," Eagle Feather warned. "Soon there will be too much light."

"I will go down there," Coyote volunteered. "I am the fastest runner."

"Couldn't we all go?" Morning Cloud suggested. "They will soon see that we are not a war party." She had already lost one child and did not want to lose another.

Eagle Feather shook his head. "It would not be wise. We have to know who they are. They could be Sarcee or even Blackfoot."

"It is not likely that the Blackfoot would come here," Deer Stalker said. "But you are right, we have to know who they are. Coyote is probably the best one to go."

He turned to his son, "You be very careful, my son. Do not take any chances. Enter the trees a good distance north of their camp and do not get too close." He was torn between his fears for his son's safety and his pride that Coyote had volunteered.

"Maybe he should take the dog," Night Star suggested.

Coyote shook his head. "He does not move quietly. Any sudden movement or sound and he would start to bark. I will be better on my own."

"They will have horses and you are afoot," Morning Cloud wailed. "They could easily run you down."

"That would be the time for you all to come charging down to rescue me," Coyote laughed. In a flash he was gone into gathering light.

They watched anxiously until he was no longer in sight.

****

Chapter V
Buffalo

Stealthily Coyote slipped into the cover of the trees some distance above where they had spotted the glow of a campfire last night. Slowly he crept forward towards the place where he figured the camp of the unknowns should be. Undergrowth was sparse in this particular grove of trees. What little there was had been partially destroyed by the fire. The boles of the trees still showed blackened scars from the big blaze.

His moccasins made no sound as he advanced swiftly from tree to tree. Soon his eyes began to pick out more details of his surroundings. The cone of a teepee came into view in the growing light. As he approached cautiously he noted that it was made of light skin, deer or elk no doubt. Certainly not buffalo! There was no sound or sign of movement anywhere around the campsite. Down on his knees now, Coyote inched forward, eyes and ears alert for any sign of life. As more of the strange teepee came into view, he saw, to his great relief, that it bore the markings of his own people, the Nakoda. Close by two horses were tethered, one of them whinnied.

On his feet now, Coyote strode boldly forward. As he neared the teepee, he called out a greeting. Suddenly the flap of the teepee opened and a man stepped out brandishing a musket which he quickly trained on Coyote.

"I come in peace, brother," Coyote said, raising his hand in the peace sign.

When the stranger heard these words in his own tongue he lowered the gun and his face broke into a smile. "You are welcome, brother," he said.

The teepee flap opened again and a young man about Coyote's age stepped out. He was followed by a woman of middle years, who Coyote guessed was his mother. Both had rather prominent front teeth.

"I am called Walking Bear," the older man told him. "And this is my woman, Nakiska, and my son Little Beaver. Our band lives south of here on Cold Water."

"I am called Coyote," Coyote told them. "My band lives on River Boiling far to the north of here."

By now the woman, Nakiska had stirred up the sleeping coals of their fire and added fresh fuel. A cooking pot appeared, which she proceeded to fill with strips of meat.

"We shot an elk," Walking Bear told his guest. "You are out early, young man. You must be hungry. Come and join us."

Coyote was hungry, partly because he had not eaten since the night before and partly because of the sudden relief of tension at finding he was among friends. He nodded happily.

He had forgotten about his family waiting anxiously on the hill above until he heard the thunder of horses' hooves coming on at a gallop.

"It is just my family," he assured his startled host who already had his gun in his hand. "I will go and greet them."

He stepped out from the shelter of the trees with a big grin on his face.

"You should have signaled to us that you were unharmed," Deer Stalker said sharply. He did not know whether to bawl his son out for not telling them he was all right or to embrace him in his relief that Coyote was unharmed.

"I was hungry," Coyote said sheepishly. "They were cooking food."

Eagle Feather snorted at this, but said nothing. Instead, he raised his arm and signaled to the women above that they could come on down.

In the meantime, Walking Bear stepped out from the trees and invited them all to come and eat with them. Soon Nakiska was adding more elk meat to the pot and explaining to the other two women how she had obtained the cooking pot from a trader who passed through their area.

Walking Bear told how they were on their way north to the River Boiling encampment of Chief Many Elk's band because they had relatives there.

"You will not have to go that far," Eagle Feather said. "We are of the Many Elk band and our main hunting camp is at Clear Water, only one sun's ride from here. What family are you related to?"

"The family of Yellow Bird," the other replied. "We are happy that we do not have to travel all the way to River Boiling. My son will be very happy to hear this. At the last big Nakoda gathering he saw a maiden from your band and was smitten by her. He has been mooning about her ever since that time."

"What is her name?" Night Star asked.

"That I do not know," Little Beaver sighed unhappily. "She and her family moved out before I could learn her name. She was very beautiful."

All three women laughed at that. "When men have stars in their eyes all women are beautiful," Nakiska smiled. "If he does not find her soon, he will become so beside himself he will be useless to us."

Eagle Feather explained that his party had come down here to see if any buffalo had come into the Ya Ha Tinda to graze on the new grass. "If the buffalo do come, a large part of our band will set up a summer hunting camp here," he said. "After all, this is Nakoda land."

"It would be good to hunt buffalo on our own land," Walking Bear nodded. "We are always courting trouble when we hunt out on the plains."

Then Eagle Feather remembered that their horses needed to be fed and watered. He beckoned to Wolf Child and instructed him to take the animals to a nearby stream two at a time and let them drink their fill. "When you asked to come with us, you were given the job of looking after the horses," he reminded his younger son. "And when that is done, I want you to tether each pair close in to the trees."

"See that you tie them well," Sun Calf grinned. "We do not want them to wander off."

"Come to think of it, he could use a little help," his father said. "You go along with him."

Reluctantly Sun Calf followed his brother over to where the horses waited, wishing that he had kept his mouth closed.

Wolf Child was only too happy to attend to the horses. It made him feel important. Horses had become very valuable to the Nakoda. If they trusted him with such valuable possessions, they must consider him to be a man or almost a man.

There were six horses in all and he and Sun Calf had just finished watering the last pair when Kakwa started to bark furiously. Wolf Child looked up and was amazed to see dark figures beginning to appear above the rim of the upper bench, which lay just south of them. More and more came, until the meadows were black with them.

Suddenly it dawned on him what he was seeing. "Buffalo!" he shouted at Sun Calf and pointed excitedly. Both boys leapt on the back of the horses they were leading and dug in their heels. The horses raced for the camp with Kakwa barking in their rear.

Hearing their cries, the others ran to the edge of the trees and stared in wonder, as hundreds of the shaggy beasts came surging up from the lower meadows along Elk River.

Eagle Feather was the first to recover. "We must get word to our band as quickly as possible." He turned to Walking Bear and said, "You may not have to travel any further. Many of our band will be coming here now. Maybe Yellow Bird and his family will be with them."

"Coyote, you should be the one to go," his father said. "You are strong and your horse is one of the best in the band."

Coyote shrugged. He did not mind going, although he would rather stay in the Ya Ha Tinda and shoot buffalo.

Then Little Beaver spoke up, "I would like to go. My horse is pretty fast too." Turning to Walking Bear he said, "You and mother can stay here and help with the buffalo hunt. I will carry the message to Many Elk. Perhaps I can persuade Yellow Bird to bring his family here to meet you."

It had occurred to Little Beaver that maybe the family of his unknown beloved would decide to remain at Clear Water to care for the old ones and he might never see her.

Coyote perked up when he heard this. It looked like he would be able to stay after all. He wondered who the maiden was who had so impressed Little Beaver. He could not think of any young women in his band who could be called beautiful. There were some pretty ones, of course. Even his cousin, Crocus, could be considered quite pretty with her slender figure and long black hair, but beautiful? Come to think of it, Crocus was a bit more than pretty. Someday perhaps he might consider doing something about that, but for now all he could think about was the coming excitement of the buffalo hunt.

Little Beaver was already busily stuffing some of the cooked elk meat into his saddle pouches as he prepared for the journey to Clear Water. Coyote told him there were plenty of small streams along the way where he could get water.

"Do not overtire your horse just because you are anxious to get there," Walking Bear cautioned his son. "Allow plenty of time for him to graze and rest."

Little Beaver cast a glance at Coyote that eloquently showed his exasperation. Would his parents ever realize that he was no longer a child?

"Tell our Chief that we think there will be enough buffalo to fill all these grasslands," Eagle Feather told the youth, as the latter prepared to mount. They all watched until horse and rider had disappeared into the forest above.

In fact they were so busy watching Little Beaver that they didn't notice the huge buffalo bull that had wandered curiously into their campsite. Walking Bear was the first to recover. He raised his musket and shot the great beast right through the chest.

"That will keep us in meat for awhile," he grinned.

Eagle Feather was impressed with the range and power of this fire stick the White Man called a gun. He noticed that Walking Bear had almost lost his balance when the weapon went off. How would this thing work if you had to fire it from the back of a horse, he wondered?

Deer Stalker and Walking Bear were already skinning the big animal and when they had finished this task the women began to cut up the meat.

Eagle Feather reminded his brother what Chief Many Elk had said about them locating their campsite farther north where the Ya Ha Tinda narrowed. They discussed the matter with Walking Bear.

"When we were here in the first Golden Eagle Moon, there were Sarcee here," he told Walking Bear. "They set fire to all the grasslands, which means they are planning to come in here and hunt. For all we know there are already Plains riders following this buffalo herd."

"We should do as your Chief advised and locate farther up the valley," Walking Bear nodded. "That makes good sense."

Overhearing this, Sun Calf turned to Coyote and said with contempt, "Sarcee, what could they do? We are more numerous than they are. Only eight of them came here before, a small hunting party. Why should we run from the Sarcee? These are our lands. There are six of us and Walking Bear has a gun."

"True, brother," Wolf Child piped up, glad to be included among the warriors. "We do not fear the Sarcee."

"Next time there might be more of them, cousins," Coyote pointed out. He grinned to himself. It amused him that these two considered themselves to be warriors.

It did not take them long to break camp. Eagle Feather and Deer Stalker and their families were already packed. Walking

Bear and his wife, Nakiska, were traveling light and were therefore able to get their things onto their travois very quickly.

As they moved off towards the upper end of the valley, they kept close to the long line of trees that ran north and south through the Ya Ha Tinda. They had little choice, by now the buffalo were beginning to fill all the grassy areas.

"We will be all right unless we cross the path of some old bull who is feeling mean and wants to fight with somebody." Eagle Feather remarked. He and his brother Deer Stalker and Walking Bear were riding together at the head of the column. Nakiska rode the horse pulling their travois while Night Star and Morning Cloud rode their own mounts. Not having a horse, Wolf Child rode on their travois, vowing that someday things would be different around here. Someday he would raid an enemy camp and steal a Chief's horse, he told himself. Sun Calf and Coyote acted as rear guards.

They chose their new campsite beside a creek at the upper end of the valley where the creek emerged from the mountains. Eagle Feather explained to Walking Bear that their Medicine Man, Otterhead, had told of a trail which led from a place near here, all the way back to where their camp was located at Clear Water.

"As soon as we are settled, we will find that trail," he said. "Then there will be no way an enemy can cut us off."

Soon their teepees were up and the women had a fire going as they set about preparing their noon meal. Wolf Child led the horses down to the stream so they could drink their fill and then he tethered them close by with enough slack so they could graze.

Coyote did not relish having to perform the many tasks that were a part of setting up camp. He preferred to be off somewhere on his horse scouting around. He considered himself to be a little above those everyday jobs that lesser people consider having to be done, which means he was a poor example for Sun Calf who idolized him.

"I will ride up onto the high ground so that I can view the whole valley," he said to his father. "Just in case there are any enemy riders following this herd."

Deer Stalker looked at his son and smiled. He knew Coyote's shortcomings when it came to work. On the other hand, he told himself, it was vital that they know if any Sarcee hunters were in the valley.

"That would be wise," he nodded, "but do not stay up there all day. There is work that must be done."

"I will go too," Sun Calf said eagerly. He, too, considered that some of the camp tasks were beneath the dignity of a true warrior.

Eagle Feather looked at his brother and grinned. "Someday these two will be great warriors, but I doubt they will ever be great workers." He gave his consent for Sun Calf to go with Coyote, although he really knew he should have told him to stay and work.

Morning Cloud, who was walking by and heard this exchange, said to Deer Stalker, "You give in too easily to Coyote's requests. The young ones must learn that there are many things in life that need to be done although they may not give much pleasure. Look at Wolf Child down there looking after the horses. He does not complain about having to work."

Eagle Feather decided that he and Deer Stalker had better get out of there before they, too, came under fire from her sharp tongue. "We had better seek Walking Bear," he said to his brother. "There is much planning that we have to do."

They found Walking Bear busily cleaning his musket. "Every time you fire one of these things it gets all dirty inside," he said. "At least you do not have to clean a bow or arrow."

Walking Bear agreed that they had much talking to do before they made their next move. For instance, would they start killing buffalo now or wait for Many Elk's hunters to arrive?

"We are not equipped to kill large numbers of buffalo," Eagle Feather pointed out. "We do not have a lot of horses and ones we have are not very fast. You, Walking Bear, can do much better than we can because you have a gun."

Walking Bear shrugged, "If it were not for you people, I would have just set out early on our journey to River Boiling and not bothered to take any buffalo. My family and I are happy to join you in this hunting. If I can kill more because of the gun, then we will share what is killed: is that not our way?"

"Before there is any big killing, we should wait until the Moose Breeding Moon, when the little ones have been weaned from their mothers," Deer Stalker said. "That is the right way to hunt. Most of the big kills are done late in the season."

"That is also when the Sarcee and maybe even their Blackfoot allies would want to come to the Ya Ha Tinda to hunt," Eagle Feather reminded his brother. "We will have to do our hunting before that time."

"This is our valley," Deer Stalker said stubbornly, "and these are our mountains."

"They would probably say that these buffalo are Plains buffalo that have wandered in here and therefore belong to them," Eagle Feather pointed out, "and that is how all conflicts begin. A skirmish with a few Sarcee is one thing, but we are not able to wage an all out war, especially with the Blackfoot."

"What we need is to find a way to kill a large number of animals in a short space of time," Deer Stalker said.

"There is such a way," Walking Bear said. "Have you not heard of the jumping pounds used by the Plains people? They drive the buffalo over a steep cliff, so that the buffalo fall to their deaths. It is not a good thing to see, but it is effective. Many do not die at once but lie wounded and have to be killed later by hand."

"I have heard of it," Eagle Feather nodded. "I, too, do not like to kill that way, but Coldmaker stays for a long time and we have many people to feed and clothe. Perhaps we will have to consider something like that."

"Where will we find such a cliff to drive them over?" Deer Stalker wondered.

"On our way up here I saw place which would do," Walking Bear told them. "It is not a cliff but a canyon. One of the creeks that flow through the Ya Ha Tinda drops away into a deep hole. When your main party arrives we will have enough riders to herd the buffalo into there. It is a long way down. The animals will surely be killed when they fall in there."

"I know that place." Eagle Feather nodded. "Tomorrow we will take a look at it, but we would have to be sure to drive only the bulls and leave the cows and calves, if that is possible."

"It might prove hard to do," Walking Bear said, "but we could try."

Coyote and Sun Calf rode in to report that all they could see out on the grasslands was buffalo. There were no signs of any hunters following them. Just then, the women called to say that the evening meal was ready.

"Come," said Eagle Feather. "We will have to talk about this later. We should have a plan ready when Many Elk and the other hunters arrive." Turning to the two youths he added, "It is fortunate that two fresh workers have arrived. There is much fuel to be gathered later to keep our night fires burning."

Sleep did not come easily that night. The great buffalo herd below them was noisy and restless. There were probably night predators skirting the edges of the herd.

Later that night both teepees were awakened by Kakwa's excited barking. Then Eagle Feather's teepee began to sway so badly that they thought it would come crashing down. Thoroughly alarmed now, they rushed out into the darkness.

****

Chapter VI

A Messenger Arrives at Clear Water

Little Beaver's excitement rose as he splashed his way across the river and rode into the big encampment. Soon he would set eyes on his beloved. To the first person he met, he announced that he had an important message for Many Elk and was directed to the Chief's lodge.

"The buffalo have come into the Ya Ha Tinda," Little Beaver blurted out as the Chief emerged from his teepee: no polite greetings, none of the courtesies that such a meeting demanded.

The Chief looked at the newcomer askance. This excited young man was a stranger to him and he wanted to know whom he was talking with. Did not this young man know that certain amenities had to be observed? He was so incensed by this that he failed to get the full import of Little Beaver's words.

Little Beaver realized he had made a breach of manners and quickly sought to make amends. "I am Little Beaver," he explained. "My father is Walking Bear of the Cold Water band. We are kin to Yellow Bird, one of your people."

The Chief was happy to hear that. Now they could proceed. The word 'buffalo' had finally sunk in. "Buffalo? You spoke of buffalo?"

"In the Ya Ha Tinda," Little Beaver nodded. "The whole valley is full of them."

"That is good news," the Chief said, "but I had expected one of my band to bring this word." A trace of suspicion had crept into his voice. "What band did you say you were from? Where are Eagle Feather, Deer Stalker and their families?"

Little Beaver began to fear that this discussion could go on all day. He was tired from his journey and wanted to get on with his quest to find his beloved. Fortunately for him his uncle, Yellow Bird, strolled over to see what all the fuss was about. On seeing Little Beaver, he rushed over and embraced him.

"This is the son of my brother-in-law, Walking Bear," he beamed at the Chief.

"Now I am really happy," Many Elk beamed back. "It is good to know when all is well. Now tell us about the buffalo, young man," he encouraged.

Little Beaver saw that he was not going to get away until he had explained everything in detail. "My family and I were camped in the Ya Ha Tinda when your people arrived there," he told them. "We were traveling north to visit you, uncle. While we were enjoying a meal together, the buffalo suddenly appeared. They came climbing up out of the river bottom until they filled all the upper grasslands. They were going to send Coyote to tell you this, but I volunteered to come in his place." He did not say why.

"You did well, young man," Many Elk nodded. Turning to Yellow Bird, he was suddenly all business. "We will have to assemble the Council. We have much planning to do. This is indeed good news for us," he enthused. "When Coldmaker comes, we will have buffalo pemmican to eat and buffalo robes to keep us warm. We must get our hunters down there as soon as possible."

Yellow Bird took his nephew aside and pointed to a teepee a short distance from where they stood. "That is the lodge of Black Wolf, who is brother to Eagle Feather and Deer Stalker, go and tell them the news. They will be anxious to hear about their families in the Ya Ha Tinda. When you have seen them, come to my lodge, which is just beyond theirs. They will point it out to you. You must be tired after your long journey. I will see that your horse gets food and water."

Just as Little Beaver reached the lodge of Black Wolf, a tall, slender young woman stepped out and looked at him enquiringly. Little Beaver stopped dead in his tracks and just stared. It was her; he was unable to believe his eyes. He started to say something, but his voice failed him: only a sort of gurgling sound came out.

Crocus began to get a little annoyed. Who was this stranger and why did he not say something? "Who do you wish to see?" she said sharply. "Is it my father Black Wolf?"

Little Beaver nodded weakly, still unable to find his voice. He could not believe that he was looking at the one he had come so far to see. Finally he recovered enough to remember his mission. "Yes," he stammered. "I bring news from the Ya Ha Tinda. The buffalo have come."

"Oh," Crocus cried happily. "The news you bring is good. My father will be very happy to hear this," but no happier than she, herself, was. Soon they would all be going to the Ya Ha Tinda and she would see her beloved Coyote.

At that moment Black Wolf emerged from the lodge and looked curiously at the newcomer.

"He bring news of the buffalo, father," Crocus cried.

"They are now in the Ya Ha Tinda?" Black Wolf asked the youth.

Little Beaver nodded. "They came soon after daybreak this morning, enough of them to fill all the upper grasslands. Coyote was supposed to bring you the news, but I said I would come instead. I think Coyote wanted to stay and hunt buffalo."

Crocus' face fell at this. She would have preferred to see Coyote.

"How are my brothers?" Black Wolf asked. "And their families, are they all well?"

Again Little Beaver nodded. "They are with my father, Walking Bear, and my mother, Nakiska. We are from the Cold Water band. As I rode off, I heard a shot. I think they had already started to kill buffalo."

"A gunshot?" Black Wolf said sharply. "My brothers do not possess a gun." This was not good. If his brothers had obtained a gun somewhere, he would no longer have the prestige that came with owning the only gun in the band. Once again he would be just their little brother.

"My father has a gun," Little Beaver explained.

In the meantime, Crocus had gone inside the teepee. Little Beaver continued to stare at the entrance flap, as if he were mesmerized by it.

Black Wolf noticed this dazed look and decided that the young man must have ridden long and hard to bring this welcome news to them. "You must be tired and hungry," he said kindly. "Have you some place to stay?"

Little Beaver was tempted to say no, but he knew his uncle, Yellow Bird, would expect him to stay with them. "I am kin to Yellow Bird. He said his lodge was near yours."

Black Wolf pointed to a teepee close by. "That is the lodge of Yellow Bird. Go now, you will need much rest after such a journey. We will talk later about the Ya Ha Tinda."

As Little Beaver made off in the direction indicated, Black Wolf stepped back inside his teepee where Keena and Crocus were busy preparing a meal under Moraha's supervision. His wife, Grey Dawn, was nursing the baby, Badger. Old Muskowa was dozing away in a corner.

"That young man must have ridden very hard," Black Wolf told them. "His mind was elsewhere as we spoke, like someone who has been hit over the head. I did not ask him where is horse was. I hope it is being cared for."

"His kinsman, Yellow Bird, would see to that," Crocus said.

"I am glad that our people are well," Grey Dawn smiled. "From what they told us about the Sarcee, I was afraid they might run into trouble."

There was a loud shout outside their teepee. Black Wolf poked his head out to see what was up. It was Moosekiller. He had been delegated to inform everyone in the band about the Council meeting that evening. He was carrying a trader's musket similar to the one owned by Black Wolf. "I got it at Old House," he said proudly.

Black Wolf's face fell. Now he was no longer the only one in the band who had a gun.

Moosekiller shook his head. "That Chief of ours cannot make up his mind whether to move the whole band down there or just take some of our best hunters and their families. There will be plenty of argument at this meeting." With that, he moved off to inform another family of these great events.

As usual, the Council lodge was packed from wall to wall. After much debate it was finally decided that only about thirty hunters would make up the party and that they would take every available horse that could be spared to serve as pack animals for the loads of buffalo meat and hides that they expected to harvest. For the most part, younger hunters would be chosen for they also had younger wives to handle the heavy chore of cutting and curing the meat and scraping the hides for drying. It was decided that only a few skin teepees would be taken and that up to three families could share a teepee until a suitable campsite could be found. Sleeping robes and cooking equipment could be carried on the packhorses. No travois would be taken because this would slow the party down. If travois were needed later, they could be easily built on the site.

"When will we leave?" one of the younger men wanted to know.

There was some debate about this; some wanted to leave the next morning, but it was finally decided it should be the day after tomorrow. "We must plan carefully for such an undertaking," the Chief cautioned. He could never be ready himself by tomorrow morning and he was still strongly resolved to go with them. It was true that he was no longer young, but youth needed to be tempered with wisdom and he decided he was the one to supply that wisdom.

As they left the meeting, old Muskwa observed that the whole business seemed pretty foolhardy to him. "There will be much wailing in the lodges after this," he predicted. "The Sarcee and the Blackfoot will come into the Ya Ha Tinda and there will be fighting and many empty saddles."

"Be quiet, old man," Moraha snapped. "You are just jealous because you will not be going."

During the meeting Grey Dawn had observed one thing that had caused her some amusement. It was the way the young man, Little Beaver, could not take his eyes off her daughter, Crocus. She remarked on this to Crocus later. "It appears that you have stolen Little Beaver's heart," she laughed.

"He looks like a beaver," Crocus sniffed. "He is not tall and handsome like my Coyote. Coyote is my man."

"Does he know that?" her mother wondered. "It seems to me that Coyote takes you for granted."

"He will know it," her daughter retorted.

"I think you would be wise to play up to Little Beaver," Grey Dawn advised. "Then perhaps Coyote will take notice of you. Sometimes men do not realize they want something until they see that someone else wants it. That is the way they are."

Keena, who was looking after the baby, Badger, was listening with interest to this conversation. "I do not think it is right to encourage someone when you are not really interested in them," she observed. She adored her cousin, Coyote, and did not want to see him deceived. On the other hand maybe Crocus would really get to like Little Beaver and then someday perhaps Coyote would begin to notice her. She was beginning to feel the faint stirrings of womanhood within herself, although she was not fully aware of it.

Keena was determined that she, too, would be a member of this hunting party. She yearned to see her family again. Anyway, if she did not go, who would look after Badger? Crocus was more than willing to leave this job to Keena and Grey Dawn would be busy cutting and curing meat.

Crocus, who was thoughtfully considering her mother's words, began to see that perhaps that Grey Dawn was right.

Coyote did seem to take her for granted. She was beginning to look forward to this journey and its many possibilities.

****

Chapter VII

The Moon of Red Berries

The camp in the Ya Ha Tinda was slowly getting back to normal since the rampaging grizzly bear had nearly destroyed one of their teepees two nights ago. It was Eagle Feather's lodge that the angry beast had attacked. Coyote was the first to recover. He went charging out with his lance and hurled it at the big, dark form that loomed over him. The lance struck it in the chest, but the grizzly still lunged at Coyote in a frenzy of anger. It took Walking Bear's gun to finally end the matter.

It was lucky that none of them had been hurt. Why Kakwa had not sensed the bear's presence and warned them, they could not understand. The big hound was the last straggler out of the teepee. As if overcome by guilt at his negligence, he set up a furious barking.

Looking at the quivering mass on the ground, Eagle Feather was more than ever convinced that a gun was a very good thing to possess.

"It must have smelled the meat and the hides," Walking Bear nodded. "It is an old bear and probably no longer swift enough to bring down an elk or deer. Young buffalo are even harder to get because they are protected by the herd."

"We can use the hide," Deer Stalker observed, "but I am not sure about the meat. I have heard that it can be pounded and then cooked with many wild onions, but I have no desire to try it."

A good part of their day had been spent cutting poles to reinforce the frames of both lodges. Before the work parties could be formed, Coyote and Sun Calf had ridden off to scout the valley for intruders. The sun was close to the rim of the western Mountains when Sun Calf came galloping back to say they had sighted a large group of riders approaching from the south.

"Coyote has gone in for a closer look," Sun Calf told them.

"I hope he will use caution as he approaches them," Deer Stalker sighed, knowing that caution was not Coyote's strong point.

"If I had thought there was any danger, I would have gone with him," Sun Calf said, a little aggrieved that anyone might think otherwise. "I distinctly saw Chief Many Elk with them."

Soon the company of riders came into view below their camp. In the vanguard, indeed, rode their worthy Chief, looking very satisfied that he had led his charges here without mishap. Beside him rode Coyote and his Uncle Black Wolf. When the proper greetings had been exchanged, the Chief noted that there were four meat curing fires burning with chunks of meat hanging over them on tripods of sticks.

"We have killed four buffalo," Eagle Feather explained. "And all but one of these was killed by Walking Bear's gun."

Chief Many Elk shook his head, "We will have to do a lot better than that. We have only three guns in our party, including the one owned by your friend, Walking Bear. We do not have the powder and bullets to kill the amount of buffalo we will need. Such things are costly and hard to get. We will have to work out a plan that will give us a bigger kill at less cost."

"We have come up with such a plan," Deer Stalker told the Chief. "It is used by the Plains people to kill large numbers of buffalo at once. They call it a jumping pound."

Eagle Feather gave Many Elk an outline of the plan. "Buffalo in large numbers are driven over a cliff," he explained.

"Most of them die when they hit the ground below. Those that survive are killed right away by people down there with lances."

"I have heard of that," Black Wolf cut in, not to be left out of the discussion. "It is messy, but large numbers are killed in a short time."

"Is there such a cliff in the Ya Ha Tinda?" Many Elk wanted to know.

"We have found such a place," said Walking Bear, who had just come up to join the group. He explained about the big waterfall and the deep canyon below it.

"That plan sounds good." The Chief nodded, "Very good. I am happy there is such a plan. Now we must gather our people together and tell them about it. There is only one thing which bothers me and that is, how do we get the buffalo to jump into the canyon?"

"We build fences leading down to the jumping point," Eagle Feather told him. "And then we herd them down."

It was decided to tell everyone of the plan after they had had their evening meal. Most of the newcomers were busy putting up pole teepees for the night. There were more metal axes in the band now so they were able to work more quickly.

Most of the party had heard of the grizzly bear attack two nights ago and wanted a good secure place to sleep.

Coyote was tired of all this labour, so he decided to seek out Crocus. He was surprised that she had not come running over to him as usual. When he did find her she was not alone; she was in animated conversation with Little Beaver. It was not really a conversation. Crocus was doing all the talking and Little Beaver was gazing at her in rapt attention.

Suddenly the truth dawned on Coyote. Crocus was the beautiful vision that Little Beaver had seen at that tribal meeting and he was now wooing her with his whole being. Words were not needed, his beaming face told it all.

Coyote turned angrily away. He did not like this one bit. Later he would have a talk with Little Beaver. Did the latter not know that Crocus was his woman? For the first time he began to see that his cousin was a very important part of his life and he was not going to let someone from another band take her away.

Out of the corner of her eye, Crocus watched Coyote stalk angrily away and smiled to herself. Maybe her mother's words were good counsel. On the other hand, maybe she should not have ignored Coyote completely. Suppose he got so angry with her that he would start looking for someone else? There were plenty of young women in the band who had an eye for Coyote. She felt a sinking feeing in the pit of her stomach and felt an urge to run after him and tell him that Little Beaver meant nothing to her. Actually she was finding the latter a little boring and he did indeed look a bit like a beaver.

Coyote strode over to where his uncle, Black Wolf, was putting up his pole teepee and offered to help him. A surprised Black Wolf lost no time in putting him to work. Coyote threw himself into the task as if his life depended on it.

That night Many Elk gathered his party together and explained the jumping pound idea to them. They were told they would have to build strong pole fences that would converge at a point just above the waterfall. Then riders would move in on the herd and try to drive selected animals into the trap. If possible the riders would drive only bulls, and leave the cows and calves alone.

"This is the only way we will be able to kill all the buffalo we need," the Chief concluded.

Well before sunup the next morning the whole camp was astir. Most of the group was sent out to cut poles for the long corral that was to be built above the waterfall.

Coyote was so busy he did not get a chance to see either Crocus or Little Beaver that day. He and Sun Calf were told to patrol the down river approaches to the Ya Ha Tinda and keep an eye out for any enemy hunters. Little Beaver was put to work hauling poles from the wooded areas down to the waterfall site. There was no time for the type of confrontation that Coyote had in mind.

Crocus was busy too. Women and children, who were not to be employed around the curing fires, were sent out to gather berries for the making of berry pemmican. Everybody had some task to perform. All would share in the bounty of hides and buffalo meat they expected to gather.

About mid-morning, Wolf Child, Keena and Crocus were busy working a berry-laden patch when Keena gave a scream of terror. A big black bear had suddenly risen out of the bushes in front of her. Kakwa had been prowling the undergrowth nearby looking for mice or rabbits to chase when he heard Keena's cry. He raced to the scene and sank his teeth in the bear's left shank.

With an angry roar the beast turned and lunged at Kakwa giving Keena and the others a chance to back away. The big claws missed Kakwa, as he leapt nimbly away. He was too smart to try and close with the bear.

As the bear turned back to the children, it found itself faced by a very determined Wolf Child, armed with a big piece of dead tree branch that he had picked up from ground. Wolf Child remembered that his father had taught him that you fight back if attacked by a black bear, but you played dead with a grizzly. When the bear lunged at him, Wolf Child swung his crude weapon with all his might and hit the bear squarely on the nose. This caught the beast by surprise and it halted for a brief moment, as if confused. Wolf Child backed slowly away still brandishing his weapon, but unfortunately for him his foot encountered another branch on the ground and he went sprawling. As Keena rushed in to help her brother, Kakwa took advantage of the opportunity to sink his teeth into the bear's other shank. Crocus picked up a piece of jagged rock and prepared to hurl it at the bear when a lance came hurtling through the air and buried itself deeply in the animal's chest.

Little Beaver stepped out of the bushes looking very pleased with himself. Crocus rushed to him and gave him a big hug for saving their lives. The other two did the same. Little Beaver went over to retrieve his spear, basking in his sudden mantle of heroism.

Kakwa was sniffing gingerly at the dead bear when a spasm caused the body to jerk suddenly and air escaping through the slack jaws made a hissing sound. Kakwa jumped back out of the way and everyone laughed. It was the laughter of relaxed tension. The uproar had drawn the attention of other berry pickers and they gathered around to view the steaming carcass. Little Beaver strode proudly off to get a horse so they could haul the carcass to their campsite.

Wolf Child, Keena and Crocus set about gathering the berries that had spilled onto the ground during the excitement. They started to pick again, but their hearts were not in it because they could not concentrate on their work for fear another bear might pop up suddenly out of the bushes.

That night tributes were piled on Little Beaver for his prowess in killing the bear. This bothered Keena when she thought of how Wolf Child had stood bravely in front of them as the bear came at them. "If my brother and Kakwa had not held the bear at bay, we would have been dead before Little Beaver arrived," she said sharply. "My brother was as brave as any warrior."

Even Little Beaver had to admit that this was true, so Wolf Child came in for quite a bit of attention, which he did not mind one bit.

Eagle Feather patted his youngest son on the back. "You will be a great hunter some day," he smiled. Night Star was proud of her son too, but inwardly she shuddered at how close her two young ones had come to death or serious injury. She thanked the Great Spirit that no harm had come to them, but she had to smile at the way Wolf Child was strutting around enjoying his moment of glory.

When Coyote and Sun Calf got back from their patrol and heard what had happened they praised him too, but Coyote's nose was a bit out of joint when he heard how Little Beaver had slain the bear and thus saved the woman of his dreams, Crocus. A black bear he sniffed, had he not hurled his lance into a huge grizzly two nights before. He figured it was time that he staked out his position as far as Crocus was concerned.

"Thank you for rescuing my woman," he said to Little Beaver in a condescending tone.

His words kind of caught Little Beaver by surprise. He knew he was no match for Coyote if it came to a fight. Coyote was bigger and stronger; he had to admit that. However, Little Beaver had no intention of backing down on this issue. At this point he figured he had just as good a chance to win Crocus as Coyote did. Had she not smiled on him the past few days?

"What makes you think she is your woman?" he retorted.

"Because that is what she is," Coyote snapped.

It might have come to blows, but at that moment Deer Stalker came up to them and told Coyote that there was something he wanted him to do. Deer Stalker did not let on that he had heard part of their argument. When he walked away his son followed obediently.

Nobody observed Crocus, who was half hidden by one of the lodges. She had heard the entire exchange. Her heart had soared when Coyote had called her for his woman, but she also did not want serious trouble to develop between the two men. She mentioned their encounter to her mother later on.

"Perhaps it would be better if you did not pay any attention to either of them," Gray Dawn advised. "It is important that we all live in harmony in this camp. There is much work that must be done here."

****

Chapter VIII

The Buffalo Jump

Grey Dawn was right. Setting up a buffalo jump involved a lot of work and it was work the Nakoda had not had much experience with. It was not as if they could go out on the plains and watch their neighbours, the Sarcee or Blackfoot, who were experts at it. They would be slaughtered along with the buffalo. The only person in the band who had seen a buffalo jump in action was Moosekiller on his journeys to visit his wife's people, the Cree. It was agreed that Moosekiller would be in charge of setting up the line of fences, which would force the fleeing buffalo into the trap.

He set about the job with gusto, shouting orders here and there and stirring everybody into action. He seemed to enjoy his newfound authority. As far as Chief Many Elk was concerned, he could have it. In many ways the Chief was just an elderly Coyote. He considered himself too old for physical labour and had never particularly enjoyed it even in his youth. Like any good politician he figured his ability to talk was his biggest asset.

The first thing Moosekiller did was to appoint crews of younger men to go out into the spruce stands and cut poles. These would be bound into travois-sized loads and hauled to the jump site. Thus, Coyote and Little Beaver found themselves engaged in a flurry of activity, which left them little time to pursue their quarrel over Crocus. When enough poles had been assembled near the top of the falls, they were told to start gathering stones to anchor the poles because the land was too rocky in most places to dig post holes.

Neither young man enjoyed the job he was doing, but Coyote consoled himself with the thought that after the trap was set up there would be the excitement and thrill of the chase.

The fence lines spread out from the top of the waterfall in the form of a vee so that the gap was narrowest at the brink of the falls and widest at the upper end where the fleeing buffalo would enter. As the frenzied animals neared the drop, they would be only three or four abreast. When the abyss appeared suddenly before them, they would be going too fast to stop and too tightly wedged to turn. The force of the charging herd behind them would force them over to their doom.

Moosekiller gave last minute instructions to the drivers. "Remember that our horses have not been trained in this," he cautioned. "They are not as swift as those of the plains people. Pick out the younger bulls and start them running and stay together at the back. I do not want to see anyone caught in the running herd and go over the rim with them. And one last thing, avoid the big old herd bulls they just might decide to turn on you and charge."

Moosekiller had barely finished talking when Coyote and several of the younger riders dug their heels into the sides of their mounts and galloped down to where the buffalo herd was grazing. Hard on his heels rode Little Beaver, anxious to prove he was just as able as Coyote when it came to stampeding a buffalo herd.

Separating the cows and calves from the bulls was not a problem. The bulls were not interested in the cows and were quite content to leave them to tend the young ones. They were concentrated down closer to the creek, which fed the waterfall. Most of the younger bulls grazed in groups of a dozen or more but the big old bulls had a tendency to wander off by themselves.

The riders approached quietly from down wind. Then at a signal from Moosekiller they broke into a gallop. Hooting and hollering, the riders bore down on a small cluster of animals at the southern end of the herd. Most of the buffalo took off south in a panic while a few escaped by splashing over the creek to the far side. There was much snorting and grunting and some bellows of protest from the stampeding herd.

"Go after those that are heading towards the jump!" Moosekiller shouted waving his gun. The others were off in a cloud of dust.

Coyote reveled in the thrill of the chase. He could smell the fear, as the frenzied buffalo fled in a great thunder of hooves. Now they were bearing down on the entrance to the trap. Lining the crude fences was a crowd of Nakodas shouting and beating sticks. Suddenly the brink was before them. As planned, those in the fore who tried to turn were shoved over by the sheer weight and momentum of those behind, who soon followed the front runners into the abyss.

The riders stopped well short of the rim, sweating, but triumphant at the success of their first drive. There was much laughing and backslapping. For the moment Coyote and Little

Beaver forgot they were supposed to be at odds with each other. Then there was a shout from Moosekiller for them to return to the herd and bring down another bunch.

"That will be the last for today," he said as he rode up to them. "We do not want to panic the whole herd. Give them a chance to settle down."

As Coyote rode back up the valley, he had an idea. It would be a feather in his cap if he was able to drive one of the old herd bulls down to the jump. That would show Little Beaver who was the best man. It would be a much bigger coup that just spearing a black bear.

While the others were moving in on a group of young bulls, Coyote set his sights on a big herd bull that stood alone just a short distance to the right of the animals targeted by his friends. This one would suit him fine, he told himself. The bull was probably old because it appeared to be just standing there half asleep. It was not even grazing, but it was massive in size. Now if he could just move in behind it without being noticed and ride up suddenly shouting as loud as he could, he figured he could startle it enough so that it would leap forward into the path of the others and be carried along with them. The old bull was already pointing in the right direction.

Digging his heels into the black mare, he urged her forward into a run "HI-YAH, HI-YAH!" he shouted.

The big bull came awake in a hurry and appeared to be moving forward to join the others when it whirled suddenly with amazing agility and aimed a thrust at Coyote's horse that would have gored her had she not suddenly reared up on her hind legs to avoid it. Even at that a glancing blow on her flank by the massive head as the bull charged past caused her to stagger back. This movement unseated Coyote and he landed on the turf with a jolting thud. His frightened mare bolted from the scene in a panic.

Shaking his head to clear his vision, Coyote started to rise slowly to his feet when he saw that the enraged bull had turned and was charging back at him. Coyote was up in a hurry and running for his life ignoring the pain in his hip caused by the fall. To his horror the bull was rapidly gaining on him. For the first time in his life Coyote was engulfed in a wave of fear and tried to increase his pace.

Just when Coyote figured he was done for, a shot rang out and the bull collapsed in a cloud of dust and lay still.

Moosekiller rode up, his gun still smoking. "I told you to stay clear of the old herd bulls!" he cried angrily. "You almost got yourself killed!" They were joined by Deer Stalker and Eagle Feather who had seen the whole thing.

"You have a lot to learn my son," Deer Stalker said severely, and could say no more because his throat was choked with emotion. He had thought for sure that his son would be gored to death before his eyes.

"To be a true warrior you first have to learn to obey orders," Eagle Feather told his nephew quietly. "Moosekiller told you to avoid the old bulls, but you thought you knew better."

As Coyote swung meekly up behind his father, he did not feel much like a warrior.

"Now we will go and find your horse," Deer Stalker said more calmly, but he was still shaken by his son's narrow escape.

They found the frightened mare halfway up towards camp, standing near a grove of poplars. She was making a few attempts to graze, but did not seem to have the heart for it. She was still trembling from her ordeal. At the sound of their approach, she jerked her head up nervously.

"Now you lead her up to camp," Coyote's father said quietly. "Do not attempt to get on her. When you get to camp give her a drink of water and then put her out to graze for the rest of the day. We will have a talk about your foolishness later." There was an ominous tone to his voice that Coyote did not like.

He approached the black mare slowly, talking soothingly to her as he advanced. She watched his approach warily, but her ears were up questioningly. Was he going to take her back among those fierce animals? When Coyote laid hold of the reins and began to walk her towards camp, she relaxed and followed him quietly.

And this is how, in the days which followed, Coyote found himself down near the base of the falls, assigned the ignominious task of putting his spear through any wounded buffalo that had somehow managed to survive the drop.

****

Chapter IX

Captured

As the summer wore on, the Nakoda hunting camp began to take on the aspects of a factory. Many curing fires burned throughout each day and the odour of smoked meat filled the air. Hides were scraped, dried, and tanned and collected into bundles for shipment back to the camp at Clear Water. Sun-dried meat was mixed with berries and pounded into pemmican. Leftover scraps were either burned or buried to keep prowling animals away from the camp. Already pack horses had carried two loads back to the home base.

Both Coyote and Little Beaver were puzzled at Crocus' apparent indifference to them, but they were kept too busy to worry much about it. They were completely unaware that there was a tacit agreement between Eagle Feather, his brothers and Walking Bear that no personal feuds must be allowed to fester that would hinder the progress of the hunt.

Two men had replaced Coyote below the waterfall to lance any animals that were not killed in the drop. Lines were attached to the carcasses that were then hauled up to the grasslands above. Many travois had been hastily constructed to haul the carcasses to camp.

Chief Many Elk wondered aloud whether the blood flowing down the creek would be lost in the swift flowing waters of Elk River or whether these stains would still be discernable to any enemy patrols farther downstream. Just to make certain that no enemy parties would surprise the workers, Coyote and Sun Calf were dispatched to patrol some distance down the river. It was also part of the plan to keep Coyote away from Little Beaver.

"What do you think of the Chief's idea that the blood from the killing area might be seen a long way downstream?" Sun Calf asked his cousin, as they rode side by side just below the rim of the upper grasslands.

"Ha, Many Elk is an old woman," Coyote scoffed. "There is lots of blood in the creek, but once it hits the river it will disappear. You will see when we get down there."

Sun Calf noticed that his horse was limping a bit. It seemed to be favouring its right front foot. He pulled up beside the trail and dismounted.

"What's the matter?" Coyote asked.

"My horse is limping." Sun Calf said. "I think there is a thorn or something in one of its front hooves."

"Could be a thorn, could be a piece of wood," the other nodded. "You should be able to pry it out with your knife. I'll ride on down to the river to look for any enemy signs and pick you up on the way back if you can't ride him. I may even find the river red with blood," he added with a laugh.

Sun Calf watched his cousin ride down into the brush covered river breaks and then he turned his attention to the injured foot. He found that a small sliver of bone had wedged itself in there and he had no difficulty dislodging it with his knife. When he looked up to see how Coyote was faring, he saw a sight that horrified him. Down below, his cousin was surrounded by six or eight riders. He could see right away that they were Sarcee warriors.

Sun Calf's first instinct was to charge down there among the intruders wielding his lance. It is what Coyote would probably have done if their roles were reversed. Then his common sense took over. If he did that, he would either end up dead or the Sarcee would have two prisoners instead of one, neither of which would be of any help to Coyote. No, his best course would be to race back to camp and raise the alarm. That is what a scout is supposed to do. Once they learned what had happened, his people would organize a war party and rescue Coyote and he would be one of them.

Sun Calf swung his horse around and rode off at full speed. His horse was running easily now that the obstruction had been removed. He did not wait to see if the Sarcee had seen him. He just dug his heels in and prayed to the Great Spirit that his head start on the enemy would get him safely into camp.

"Coyote has been taken prisoner," he shouted at the first person he encountered on the edge of the camp. It happened to be his uncle, Black Wolf. Soon Sun Calf was surrounded by a crowd of excited people, including his father, Eagle Feather, and Chief Many Elk.

"This is bad news. It could mean real trouble for us," the Chief said. "How many Sarcee were down there young man?"

"Six or eight, I am not sure," Sun Calf told him. "My first thought was to rush down to Coyote's aid; I do not like to flee from an enemy. Then I decided that this would be foolish and would not help Coyote. My first duty was to warn the camp."

"You acted wisely, my son," Eagle Feather said proudly. "What we must now do is organize a rescue party and we must do it at once before the enemy gets too far away."

"We must do more than that," the Chief told him. "We must start to pack up this camp in case we have to move in a hurry. We do not know how many Sarcee are in the vicinity. In fact, I think it would be wise if we moved out at once. We have all the meat and hides we need."

Deer Stalker came rushing up to them. "Is it true?" he cried. "Has Coyote been captured?"

Eagle Feather nodded gravely, "Yes, brother, it is true."

Morning Cloud who arrived at the same time as her husband let out a moan of anguish, "I have already lost one child. Must I lose the only one I have left?"

Crocus arrived a moment later. When she heard the news she rushed over to Morning Cloud to console her, but her own face was white as a sheet. Not Coyote, she prayed inwardly, please let him be saved.

"We are going after them as soon as we can get our things together," Eagle Feather assured them. "It is almost dusk now;

perhaps they will camp for the night a short way down river." He knew, though, as he said this that he was clutching at straws.

Deer Stalker ran off to get his horse and weapons. When he returned Eagle Feather and Black Wolf were already armed and mounted. The former had his hunting bow and lance and Black Wolf had his precious gun. He also had one of the new hatchets in his belt. Moosekiller came galloping up and said he would join them.

"Let me go too," Crocus begged them. "Coyote might need me if he is hurt."

"You will do better to stay here and be of comfort to Morning Cloud," her father said kindly.

By now quite a lot of people surrounded them, offering advice and wishing them well.

Listening to Crocus' words, Little Beaver knew that his case was hopeless. There was no doubt now where Crocus' heart lay.

They all stood mutely as the rescue party rode off into the gathering dusk. Then a single voice broke the silence; "May the Great Spirit ride with you," someone shouted after them.

****

Chapter X

The Prisoners

Coyote fought off his captors as long as he could, but there were seven of them and all were fairly big men. They soon had him down and then bound his hands behind him. They left his legs free until they had him back in the saddle of his horse and then these were secured as well. Apart from a few grunts, his grinning captors said very little.

Coyote cursed his carelessness in not being alert enough to have sensed the presence of danger, especially when his enemies had been so close. His thoughts had been on Crocus as he rode away from Sun Calf down into the river breaks. At least the Sarcee had not killed him on the spot, as the Blackfoot would probably have done. He wondered what they were going to do with him now that they had him trussed up like a turkey ready for the roasting spit.

Their leader was a tall warrior, who rode a big grey stallion. Coyote looked at the powerful animal with envy. One look at those heavy shoulder muscles and the long legs told him that here was a prize worth taking. If he had a horse like this, nobody would be able to catch him. The problem was how was he going to get from his horse onto the back of the stallion when his hands and feet were tied and there were seven burly warriors around him?

The horse's owner rode up beside Coyote and spoke to him haltingly in the Nakoda tongue. "How many men are in your party?" Coyote considered this for a moment. If he said only a few, the Sarcee would not send in a big party to attack them and his people would be able to overcome them. He was sure that attack was what these warriors had in mind. On the other hand, if he said his whole band was in the Ya Ha Tinda, these riders might fear for their own safety and rapidly leave the area, taking him with them. He had to make them believe there was no immediate danger threatening them. Darkness was coming; maybe his captors would camp nearby.

A sharp clout on the side of his head told him that the big man did not intend to wait long for an answer.

"We are twelve hunters and their families," he said.

"Why did you come here to hunt our buffalo?" was the next question.

"Because the Ya Ha Tinda is Nakoda country," Coyote said proudly, "and we hunt any animals we find here."

This brought him another clout on the head, which he took disdainfully. He was not about to cower before his captors.

The big Sarcee glowered at him for a moment then rode off to the head of the column.

They were moving down river at a brisk pace now. It was evident to Coyote that these people were not going to camp for the night. They were headed for a Sarcee camp somewhere downstream. It could not be too far away because these men were not equipped for a long journey. The question was how big was this Sarcee camp?

The sun was very low in the sky now. It could just be seen in a narrow gap between the mountains. The next moment it disappeared into gathering clouds. It was evident that a storm was approaching. A steady rain began to fall drenching them all. Tempers began to flare. Horses stumbled on the wet stones of the river. As darkness fell, their pace slowed to a walk.

Before long, a big mountain with a humpback top loomed dimly on their right, its outlines barely discernable. Coyote knew this mountain marked the gateway to the Ya Ha Tinda. At this point Elk River spilled out into a series of low foothills. His captors became more cheerful so he sensed they must be nearing the Sarcee camp. The rain continued to pour down. They sloshed their way across the river at a point where the stream widened into a series of gravel bars and then rode up onto a flat grassy meadow. Coyote could see the glow of campfires ahead. He would soon know his fate he told himself.

Coyote was anxious to see the size of this encampment. If it were not a large camp, it would be easier for him to be rescued. He was sure his people would send a party after him. Sun Calf would have lost no time in getting back to tell them of his capture. Perhaps even now they were somewhere in the darkness behind him. If this camp was a large one it, would be a different story. It would mean heavy fighting and many of his people would be killed.

The rain had stopped as quickly as it had started and a brisk wind sprang up that pushed thunder storm clouds off to the east. They had reached the perimeter of the Sarcee camp now: its teepees looming ghost-like in the dark. It was not a big camp or a very permanent one. Coyote estimated there were no more than twenty lodges here, if that many.

People began to gather around them as they passed the first teepees. There were a few derisive shouts when they caught sight of Coyote, who was a sorry sight, wet from head to toe and lashed to his horse. Some of the bolder children threw a few rocks but none of these hit him.

These were not people who were full of anger and hatred. Their men were safely home; nobody had been killed or wounded.

The leader dismounted in front of a brilliantly decorated lodge and tossed his reins to a young woman, who had emerged from the dwelling. She gave Coyote a quick appraising glance.

"Nakoda," the man said, pointing to Coyote. "They are hunting our buffalo up in the Ya Ha Tinda.

He motioned for two of his men to lift Coyote from his horse. They undid the thongs which bound his legs and lifted him to the ground so that he could walk. They led him to a small teepee some distance away. Coyote could hear the neighing of horses and could just discern the outlines of a crude corral off to the right. His captors pushed him inside none too gently. One of them spoke to him but he did not understand what was said. They left him then, laughing to each other as they went.

Coyote took note of his surroundings. It did not appear that this teepee was being used as a dwelling. Several bundles of elk hide were strewn about. The Sarcee's had apparently enjoyed good hunting. He sat down on one of the bundles to consider his situation. He was tired, wet, and hungry and there did not seem to be much hope that he could loosen his bonds and escape. On the other hand, his situation was not entirely hopeless. This was a small camp and there were enough of his people to overcome his captors.

It all depended on Sun Calf. Coyote knew his cousin would not be foolish enough to try to trail the Sarcee to their camp. He would head back to warn the others, but was his horse's foot healed enough so that Sun Calf could ride him? If not, Sun Calf would have to lead his mount all the way back.

Suddenly he heard voices outside the teepee, a man and a woman talking. The flap of the lodge was tossed aside and a short, stocky man stepped in, holding one of those smelly lights the traders sold. This man had not been one of the party that had captured him. He was quickly followed by the young woman who had taken the reins of the leader's horse. She was carrying a dish of hot meat.

"I have some elk meat here," she smiled. "But you will not be able to eat it unless your hands are free."

Coyote was surprised to hear her speak so fluently in his own tongue.

She turned to the short man and spoke to him sharply. He just shook his head and laughed. Obviously he had no intention of freeing Coyote's hands. As they argued, the light cast moving weird shadows on the teepee wall.

"I will have to feed you like a child," she said to Coyote, and there was a hint of amusement in her eyes. "This one here," she indicated the man beside her, "is too afraid to loosen your hands, lest you overpower him and get away."

Coyote opened his mouth and pretended to chew. He looked so funny she burst out laughing. She looked so pretty and her laughter was so infectious that Coyote burst out laughing too.

This brought an angry exclamation from the guard. Whatever he said appeared to anger the young woman. She turned on him and gave him a tongue-lashing then pointed to the open teepee flap.

He stormed angrily outside, leaving the smelly White Man's light smoking on the dirt floor.

"What did you say to him?" Coyote asked her.

"I told him that if he was afraid to untie your hands for him to go and get Lone Eagle. Lone Eagle is the leader who led the scouting party which captured you."

"The one with the big grey stallion?" Coyote's eyes shone, as he recalled watching the smooth gait of the big horse. "What I wouldn't give to own a horse like that."

She nodded, "That one is called Silver Runner. These Plains people worship their horses and give them names like people. One of my tasks is to look after him."

"I am not Sarcee," she said quickly. "I am of the Cold Water Nakoda. I was captured some years ago and am owned by the Lone Eagle family. I am called Dove."

"Have you never wanted to escape and return to your own people?"

Sudden tears filled her eyes. "I would love to return to my people," she whispered. "I have often thought of just getting on

Silver Runner and running away. They do not have another horse that could catch me, but even if I did, I would not know which way to go."

Coyote felt a surge of hope at her words. "I know the way to go. Maybe we…….."

He was halted by the sound of footsteps approaching. She held her finger to her lips. Lone Eagle stepped into the teepee. He was accompanied by another Sarcee as big as himself, who then proceeded to untie Coyote's hands. "You will be freed so you can eat," Lone Eagle said. "Then you will be tied up again. I would advise you to make no effort to escape. As you can see, White Bear is big and strong."

At the sound of his name the big warrior grinned, although he did not know what was said.

Lone Eagle explained to him what he had said and the grin widened. After a few more words with White Bear the leader strode to the doorway and disappeared.

For a moment there was only the sound of Coyote eating. Then Dove spoke softly, "Sometimes the hope of escape is all that keeps me from despair."

Coyote stopped his chewing for a moment and looked at her intently. "If the chance arises for me to escape, I will take it," he said quietly. "I do not know what plans they have for me."

Dove was about to say something else when White Bear gave her a clout and muttered what appeared to be a threat. Apparently he did not like them talking when he did not know what was being said.

Coyote could see now why she was anxious to escape. Captives did not have much status in any band. Dove was no more than a slave to the Sarcee.

As Coyote ate in silence, he became aware of a rising level of sound in the camp. There was much chanting and beating of drums. He looked enquiringly at Dove, but she decided to hold her tongue. When he had finished, he handed her the dish that she had brought the food in. He decided to risk a few words. Maybe White Bear would think he was just thanking her.

"What is all that noise?" he asked.

"A big celebration," she said hurriedly, glancing at White Bear. "Remember big celebrations lead to big sleeps." The last was followed by a meaningful look at the entrance.

White Bear growled something, but did not hit her again. He just pointed to the teepee door. It was obvious that he wanted her out of there before she and Coyote could do any more talking. He then retied Coyote's hands and left, taking the smelly light with him. Coyote had heard that the traders at Old House had such lights, but it was the first time he had ever seen one.

After they had gone, he pondered Dove's last words and the look she had given him. She had talked about 'big sleeps' at the end of the celebrations. From what she had said earlier, she had long dreamed of getting away from the Sarcee, but did not know the way back to her people. Now that he was here, maybe she had renewed hope of making her escape. Well, he could sure take her back to her people because some of them were now with his own band in the Ya Ha Tinda.

The big question after how, was when? Did she have some plan that would see them away from here before daybreak? He sure hoped that she did. There was nothing he could do but wait and see what developed.

Coyote was feeling much better now. The rain had not penetrated his buckskins, his hair had dried and his stomach was full. He wondered about the cause of the celebrations outside. He hoped it did not include taking him out there to torture and deride.

Nobody came to get him and he began to doze off. Sometime later he awoke with a start. How long had he been asleep? It was now dead quiet outside. Did he imagine it or was there a light tapping sound coming from the back area of the teepee? Yes, it was a definite tapping. He roused himself and slid off the bale of hides he had been resting on. Quickly he made his way over to where the sound was coming from.

"Who's there?" he whispered.

"Dove," a whisper came back at once. Then Coyote heard the sound of a knife cutting into the tough elk hide of the teepee wall. When she had made the opening large enough, Dove slipped through. It took her only a moment to cut the thongs that bound him. "Come quickly," she whispered, as she went back through the long slit in the wall. He lost no time in following her through.

"Close by is the corral where all the horses are kept," she whispered. "I have a horse saddled and ready."

Not a sound came from the rest of the camp, except an occasional snore as they passed a few teepees. Campfires had subsided to a few exploding sparks and glowing embers.

They managed to reach the corral without waking anyone and slipped through. With her hand on his arm she led him over to where a big horse was tied to a rail. "Silver..." Coyote started to exclaim, but she clamped a hand over his mouth.

"Take down the rails quietly," she whispered, pointing to the loose rails which barred the entrance.

She had already untied Silver Runner and was leading him towards the entrance just as Coyote pushed the last rail aside. As she passed through, he began to put the rail back.

"No, no," she whispered fiercely. "Now follow me. We must go quickly."

She chose a route that took them away from the cluster of teepees and towards the river. When they had reached the edge of the water, she stopped. "We can ride now," she said.

As Coyote moved to swing up onto the saddle, the horse reared, but Dove held the reins tightly. "If you try to ride him, he will throw you off," she told him. "I will mount him and you will get on behind me."

This was a new experience for Coyote. It did not seem right to be riding behind a woman. A man's place was in the saddle.

Dove suddenly began to laugh, partly because of the look on his face, but mostly from the relief of the tension she had endured planning their escape. "It is so good to be free," she exulted.

"We won't be able to say we are free until we are back home with our people," Coyote cautioned, which was unusual because caution was not in his nature. "Even as we speak, they might have caught some horses and are preparing to come after us."

She laughed again, "I told you they had no horses that can catch Silver Runner, even though he carries two of us."

Slowly they made their way across the river and up onto the bank on the other side. Suddenly they heard a splashing in the river behind them and the sound of hooves clattering over a gravel bar.

"Get going," Coyote hissed. "They are after us already!"

In a panic now, Dove dug in her heels and the big grey sprang forward. Coyote had to put his arms around her to keep his seat. Ordinarily this might have been a pleasant experience, but now all he could think of was escape. They could not even gallop because of the darkness and the uncertainties of the trail ahead, part of which would involve traveling across gravel bars, he remembered.

Glancing back fearfully he saw a lone horse pass through a patch of moonlight. It was riderless and there was something very familiar about its gait. With a laugh he grabbed Dove's arm and told her to stop.

"It's my horse," he grinned. "When we left the corral open it was natural for her to head for home."

"You wanted to close it," she reminded him.

As Dove brought the stallion to a halt, Coyote slipped off its back and was on the ground waiting as the black mare trotted up. She had no saddle, but that did not bother Coyote. He had often ridden her bareback. He climbed up onto her back and dug in his heels and they were off. Silver Runner did not seem to mind having a companion at all.

"We will have to go with care," Coyote warned Dove. "I have been over this trail and it is rough."

She tossed her head. "If we have to move carefully, so will any pursuers."

Coyote was not so sure. "Lone Eagle will be so angry at losing his favorite horse that he might throw caution to the winds and come racing after us. He knows this trail better than we do."

A faint glow in the east told them that dawn was rapidly approaching. Soon they would be able to make better time. Already the bushes and trees around them began to assume ghostly shapes.

They were crossing a wide river bar now, riding side by side. The hoof beats of their horses ringing loudly in the morning air.

"Yes, Lone Eagle will be very angry," Dove said soberly, as if realizing for the first time the seriousness of their situation. "If we are caught, they will beat us. They might even kill me for letting you loose and taking Silver Runner."

"If we are chased, you ride on ahead," Coyote said kindly. "You have the fast horse. After a time you will come to a big open area. Look then to the right and you will see that the land rises up steeply to the upper grasslands of the Ya Ha Tinda.

Ride north to the valley's end and you will find the camp of our people. You will be safe then. We outnumber the Sarcee about two to one."

They had left the river now and were following a rough trail. The ground was still soft from the rain of the night before, so the hoof beats of their mounts made no sound.

But there *was* sound. From somewhere behind them, they could hear the clatter of hooves on loose gravel, made all the noisier because of the speed at which the riders were traveling.

In dismay Coyote and Dove urged heir horses to a faster pace. There was not much point in using caution now. They had to keep well ahead of their pursuers, if possible. Neither of them was armed so they would be helpless against their enemies.

As they rounded a bend in the trail, Dove suddenly shouted a warning cry, their path ahead blocked by four mounted warriors. She glanced fearfully at Coyote only to find him grinning broadly. "They are Nakoda," he told her. "We are safe now."

They drew up beside the waiting riders and Coyote shouted, "We are being pursued."

Deer Stalker gave a shout of joy at seeing his son safe and sound, Eagle Feather, Black Wolf, and Moosekiller all had big grins on their faces.

"Coyote not only escaped, but he brings a pretty woman with him," Moosekiller laughed.

"How many pursuers?" Eagle Feather asked. He, too, wondered about the presence of the young woman.

Coyote shook his head. "We do not know, but they will be here soon." As he spoke, they could hear hoof beats approaching from down river.

"You two ride on home,' Eagle Feather said quickly. "You will meet more of our people on the way. We will soon have a large force here." Again he looked enquiringly at Dove, still seeking an explanation.

"This is Dove," Coyote told them. "She is Nakoda and she set me free. She is riding the favorite horse of Lone Eagle, a Sarcee Chief."

"Go then," his uncle ordered. "We will handle your pursuers." Coyote and Dove wasted no time obeying Eagle Feather's order. They took off at a gallop.

Coyote was very happy to see that there were two guns in the rescue party. As far as he knew, the Sarcee had no guns.

With the two young people out of the way, Eagle Feather and his friends moved off the trail and into the shadows of the trees. Quietly they waited for the enemy to appear.

Deer Stalker shook his head sadly, "My son is a great one for getting into trouble, but did he have to steal a chief's horse?"

"And probably the Chief's woman too," Moosekiller chuckled. He had always liked Coyote's spirit.

There was no more time for talk for the pursuers suddenly burst into view. There were only two of them, which rather disappointed Moosekiller.

"No doubt the one on the lead horse is Lone Eagle," Black Wolf said.

"He probably hoped to catch Coyote and Dove before they reached the Ya Ha Tinda." Eagle Feather nodded.

"What will we do?" Moosekiller asked. "Shall we kill them or take them prisoners?"

"Neither," Eagle Feather said. "As prisoners, they would be nothing but trouble for us. If we kill them, it would stir the

Sarcee into frenzy and we would have an all out battle on our hands. It would be wiser to just scare them."

He touched Black Wolf's arm. "Put a shot over their heads, brother. That should halt them in their tracks."

True enough, at the blast of the musket, the two riders jumped off their mounts in a flash and disappeared into the surrounding trees, dragging their mounts with them.

"Now what will we do?" Deer Stalker wondered. "We do not want a standoff. Shall we creep up on their position and force them to retreat?"

"And invite an arrow?" Eagle Feather shook his head. "Let them try to creep up on us, if they dare. I don't think they will. They know we have a gun. Right now they are probably wondering how many of us are here. If we fired two guns, I think they would head back down river in a hurry. They might come back with reinforcements of course."

"Then we could be in trouble," Deer Stalker pointed out. "Suppose our own people do not arrive in time?"

"Gun powder is too valuable to waste on thin air," Moosekiller said sourly. "We should have killed them."

Their dilemma was solved by a shout from the river. When they turned they saw about fifteen of their people riding through the river shallows. Their reinforcements had arrived. At the head of the party was Yellow Bird.

Eagle Feather explained the situation to him and he immediately sent three of his men to reconnoiter the enemy position. "Do not expose yourselves," he cautioned.

"We cannot linger here," Eagle Feather said to Yellow Bird. "We have to get back to our camp as soon as possible and talk to Coyote and the woman, Dove. We must know just how big this Sarcee camp is and where it is located. I have an idea it is not very far away and not a very big camp, because the parties they send out are so small, but we have to be sure."

Yellow Bird nodded, "And we also have to know if there are any bigger camps in the area that could reinforce them."

"Suppose they had some Blackfoot allies close by," he added. "Then we would be in trouble. We would have to move out of the Ya Ha Tinda in a hurry."

Eagle Feather agreed. "That's what Many Elk fears. He does not want us to provoke an all out war. It would be the end of us. That is why we have to talk to Coyote and the woman without delay."

At that moment the three riders that Yellow Bird had sent down river came riding back. "There was no sign of anyone," one of them reported.

With that the whole party turned and headed up the river at a brisk pace.

They did not know that from a vantage point high up in the forest, Lone Eagle was watching their every move. The Sarcee leader was somewhat dismayed at the size of this war party. He and his companion had intended to find the Nakoda camp and sneak in under cover of darkness to rescue Silver Runner, but now it appeared that this Nakoda hunting party was bigger than he had been led to believe. He silently cursed that young Nakoda captive who had deceived him.

****

Chapter XI
Bad News

"There are two riders coming up the valley," Sun Calf said to his mother, Night Star, who was preparing their morning meal. "I think I will ride down and see who they are."

"You go and help Wolf Child carry in some firewood," she retorted. "You are always riding off somewhere and leaving your brother to do all the work. Whoever is coming will arrive here without any help from you."

"Suppose they are enemies," Sun Calf said.

"Two enemies?" his mother scoffed. "I'm sure our warriors could take care of them."

But Sun Calf kept his eyes trained on the approaching riders. Suddenly he let out a whoop of joy. "It's Coyote!" he cried, "and he has a woman with him."

"Coyote?" Night Star said, with a sigh of relief. "Then he is safe after all."

Sun Calf raced over to Black Wolf's lodge, all thoughts of hauling wood banished from his mind. "Crocus!" he shouted. "It is Coyote and he has someone with him."

With a prayer of thankfulness to the Great Spirit for heeding her prayers, Crocus joined her cousin and they ran to the edge of the encampment. By this time the whole camp was aroused and faces began to appear as teepee flaps were hastily thrown open. Then Chief Many Elk arrived on the scene and strode over to where Crocus and Sun Calf were standing. He peered anxiously down the valley.

"If Coyote is here, where is the rest of the party we sent to rescue him?" he wanted to know.

As Coyote and Dove rode up, several people gasped at the beautiful stallion that Dove was riding. Crocus' face darkened when she saw that Coyote was accompanied by a very pretty young woman. Her emotions wavered between joy that he was safe and a deep fear that he may have found someone else and would no longer want her.

Morning Cloud got to her son first. As he slid to the ground, she gave him a big hug. She had given him up for lost when she had heard that he had been captured by the Sarcee. Coyote basked in all the attention he was getting.

Dove just remained in the saddle beaming at everyone who gathered around to admire her horse. At last she was back with her own people.

Coyote's eyes were fastened on Crocus in such a way that she knew that she did not have to worry about the strange woman he had brought with him. She was his woman. She knew that now beyond a shadow of a doubt.

When Coyote introduced Dove to them all, Crocus greeted her with a radiant smile, especially when Coyote told her how Dove had cut his bonds and led him from the enemy camp. "There is no way I could have escaped on my own," he said.

"Tell me about this camp," Chief Many Elk bellowed. "That is what we need to hear. How far away is this camp and how many teepees are there?"

"It is not a big camp," Coyote told him. "I would say there are less than twenty teepees. As far as warriors go, we outnumber them by two to one and Dove says they have no guns, but they are much too close to the Ya Ha Tinda for my liking. Their camp is just outside the last range of mountains."

"Your liking!" Many Elk snorted. "I would say they are too close for anyone's liking, but you say it is a small camp and we are much stronger than they are. That is good news."

Dove spoke out now, still perched proudly in the saddle of the big horse. "It is not the Sarcee that we should worry about; it is the big Blackfoot camp just one sun's ride down river. I think it is there for a purpose. I heard talk of a plan afoot for them to come in here and attack you. They say you are hunting Blackfoot buffalo."

"Now that is very bad news," the Chief admitted, his face darkening, "very bad news indeed. You say one sun's ride? How long do you think it would take them to form a party and come here? How much time do we have?"

"We talked about this as we rode here," Coyote told him. "We figured we could count on only two suns at the most."

"I am more concerned about the least, not most," Many Elk said gloomily. "Maybe we have only one sun, even less. The Blackfoot might already be on their way up here for all we know. I am going to plan on the idea that we have no time."

Walking Bear, Little Beaver and Nakiska were looking at Dove intently as she dismounted. "Coyote said you are Nakoda," Walking Bear said. "What is your band?"

"The Cold Water Band," she told them. "The Sarcee took me away when I was much younger, when they raided our camp. I was not near my family when they came; I was down by the river."

Walking Bear nodded excitedly. "I remember now, you were of the Sounding Wind family. There was much sorrow in the lodge of your parents when you were taken. You must come and stay with us. We will be returning to Cold Water soon. There will be much joy among us all when you are returned to your family."

"I would say that you should make that very soon, Walking Bear," Chief Many Elk advised him.

Coyote glanced over towards the corral, "Where are all the horses?" he asked the Chief. "On their way home," the Chief told him. "When you were taken, I feared we might be attacked at any moment, so I sent all the spare horses and the travois we had back to Clear Water with most of our meat and hides. I sent them by the trail that leads through the mountains that Otterhead told us about. That way they will be safe from attack."

Coyote had to admit that this was a sound move.

Dove was standing and talking excitedly to the Walking Bears and still holding the reins of Silver Runner.

"I will take Silver Runner over to the corral for you," Coyote suggested to Dove. "You have much to talk about."

She laughed merrily. "I do not think he will go with you. Remember when you tried to mount him?"

"Oh, I think he will come with me now," Coyote smiled. He had just noticed how the big stallion quivered whenever Coyote's black mare was near him. A plan had begun to form in his mind. If he was lucky, maybe someday he would have a fine horse of his own.

Much to Dove's surprise he was right. When Coyote approached leading his mare, Silver Runner was only too happy to be led away to the corral. As Coyote closed the corral gate on them, he chuckled to himself. Then he walked back to join the group.

"Some riders are coming," Wolf Child shouted and pointed down the valley. He and Keena had been standing there for some time taking in all the excitement that was building around them.

"It is our father returning with the war party," his sister said. "Do you not recognize his horse?"

Keena had been watching Crocus intently. Her cousin seemed to be in a very happy mood and did not seem to resent the fact that Coyote had ridden up with another woman. Keena had expected fireworks for sure. When she turned back from looking at the approaching riders, she found that Crocus had disappeared. A moment later she caught a brief glimpse of her as she slipped behind a teepee with Coyote. The mothers of the pair had noticed this, too. Grey Dawn and Morning Cloud smiled knowingly at one another.

Chief Many Elk sighed with relief. "I am happy that they are returning and that nobody is chasing them. We have much to talk about and much to do."

Eagle Feather and his brothers and Moosekiller were the first to arrive. They were soon joined by Yellow Bird and his party. The new arrivals were told about the possible threat from the Blackfoot.

"You were wise to send our meat and hides back to Clear Water," Eagle Feather told the Chief, "and wise to choose the route through the mountains. I think we should make plans to follow them soon, perhaps as soon as dawn tomorrow."

"I agree," Many Elk nodded, "but I would say a lot sooner than that." Like old Muskwa, the Chief was a bit of a pessimist.

Eagle Feather strode over to where the Walking Bear family and their kin, the Yellow Birds, were talking quietly together. Dove was with them. She had adopted the Walking Bears as her own. It felt so good to be with her own people again that she felt like singing. No one was happier to see her as part of his family than Little Beaver. He was already gazing at her with the same calf eyed look that he once bestowed on Crocus.

"My good friend," Eagle Feather said to Walking Bear, "we had had much good hunting together, but now I feel that it is time for us to part. I think you should leave at once. The Sarcee, Lone Eagle, is a very strong and determined man, from what my nephew tells me and you have his favorite horse."

Walking Bear nodded and so did the Yellow Birds. They had been discussing this very matter when Eagle Feather came up.

"We plan to leave at once and head directly to the west rim of the valley," Walking Bear told him. "We will stay very close to the mountains until we reach Elk River. We will be in the shelter of the trees most of the way. Once we are headed up river we will be safe. We will be deep within the mountains before dark."

"It will be bad for Dove if she is ever recaptured," Eagle Feather reminded them.

"I am not afraid of this Lone Eagle," Little Beaver said contemptuously. "And my father has a gun."

"Once I am on Silver Runner, nobody will be able to catch me," Dove said with all the confidence of youth.

Word spread quickly throughout the camp that the Walking Bears were leaving as soon as they could get their things together and that Dove and the stallion would be going with them.

Coyote was sitting with Crocus just outside the Black Wolf teepee when he heard that the Walking Bears were leaving right away. He was hoping that his mare would have had more time to get acquainted with Silver Runner.

"I was hoping that Dove would not leave so soon," he said ruefully.

"You told me that you did not care for Dove," Crocus said sharply. Coyote was her man now and she had no intention of sharing him with Dove or anyone else.

Seeing a coming storm, Coyote quickly explained that it was not Dove that he wanted to stay, but Silver Runner. He told her how he had put his mare in with the big stallion in the hope that they would mate.

"I thought I might as well use Silver Runner while he was here and maybe sometime around the first Moon of the Golden Eagle I would have a fine colt to raise," he said.

Her suspicions gone, Crocus burst out laughing. "I can see now that you are a devious one. I will have to keep an eye on you all the time to see what scheme you are cooking up in that handsome head of yours."

"Well, it did seem like a good idea to me," he said defensively.

"It was sound thinking," Crocus admitted. "But Dove and the Walking Bears have to move quickly, for they will be in great danger as long as they remain here. From what you told me the horse's owner, Lone Eagle, will stop at nothing to get Silver Runner back and what about Dove herself? He will do his best to get her back so he can punish her."

They got up and joined the crowd that had gathered around the Walking Bears to see them off. Out on the grasslands of the Ya Ha Tinda all was serene. The great buffalo herd was grazing quietly, which was a good sign that no intruders were in the vicinity.

Dove was astride the big stallion and appeared to be anxious to get going. Little Beaver was close beside her and to Crocus' amusement he seemed to be as enamoured of Dove as he had been of her. Only Walking Bear and his wife, Nakiska, seemed to be reluctant to part with their new friends. Nakiska had struck up a warm friendship with Night Star and others.

Dove swung Silver Runner over to where Coyote and Crocus were standing. "Thank you for bringing me back to my people, Coyote," she said and there were tears in her eyes.

"It was you who saved me," Coyote reminded her.

"We saved each other then," she laughed and she was off to join the others, riding towards the distant mountains of the western rim of the valley.

"May the Great Spirit ride with them," Chief Many Elk said solemnly. "And may he also ride with us on our homeward journey."

****

Chapter XII

Pursued

Chief Many Elk stood staring after the Walking Bears until they had disappeared from sight. Maybe he and his party should be leaving too. Was it wise to wait until the morning? The sun was only midway up in the sky. There was lots of time still left in this day. Was it wise to waste it? He looked over to where Yellow Bird was talking with Eagle Feather and his two brothers and decided to join them.

"You know, I do not feel good about this day," the Chief said. "The sky is clear, the sun shines warmly upon us and below in the grasslands the buffalo graze quietly, but I do not feel good about it."

"You think we should leave right now, don't you?" Eagle Feather said. Many Elk nodded. "We are not a war party. Our wives and our children are here with us. If the Blackfoot should come, they could slaughter all of us. They do not like us, remember. Always they have looked upon us as intruders in their land. Now, we have had a good summer. We have much meat and many buffalo robes. Why are we still here?"

"This is Nakoda land," Yellow Bird pointed out. "We have a right to be here."

"Right is fine," the Chief agreed. "It is good to be in the right, but might is better."

"What the Chief says makes sense," Eagle Feather nodded. "We can muster about thirty two warriors at best. The Blackfoot could send one hundred or more in here and still fight a major battle elsewhere."

"Moosekiller and I have guns," Black Wolf said. "We are not helpless children."

"Guns," Deer Stalker snorted. "You fire once and by the time you reload a hundred arrows have found you." He was still a bit resentful of the fact that Black Wolf had the only gun in the family.

"We have bows and arrows and our lances and knives," Yellow Bird added.

Many Elk shook his head stubbornly, "I say our families should start right out right now and if you are wise, you will follow soon after."

"I agree with the Chief," said Eagle Feather. "We may yet have to fight, who knows, but if we took the mountain trail, the enemy would have to come at us in a narrow ravine. They could not surround us and we would be between them and our families. If we tried to fight them here in the open, we would be finished."

Eagle Feather's counsel carried a lot of weight in the band. Had he not led them to the best hunting they had had in years? If Eagle Feather decided that the Chief's words were wise, maybe it would be the right thing to do. They dispersed through the camp and spread the news. Everyone was to pack up at once and leave as soon as they were ready. The whole camp suddenly became a hive of activity. There was really not much to pack because most had been getting things together ever since the day before, when Coyote had been captured.

"I am happy that we are leaving," Night Star said to Grey Dawn and Morning Cloud. "I do not feel good about this place now that the Sarcee know that we are here."

Keena and Wolf Child were happy that they were going back to Clear Water because they had a lot of friends they had not seen all summer. Sun Calf wondered how he was ever going to be accepted as a warrior if he did not have experience in battle. At least he had convinced himself that this is how he felt. Coyote would never run away from battle.

As for Coyote himself, he was of two minds. He did not want anything to happen to his family or Crocus, but he still remembered his humiliation at the hands of Lone Eagle who had cuffed him a couple of times.

The Nakoda were a nomadic people. Soon the whole encampment was on the move, strung out in a long single line. The vanguard had already disappeared into the ravine where the creek poured out into the Ya Ha Tinda. There was no time to try to erase all signs that there had been a camp here. That would have been a mighty task considering all the meat curing and hide scraping that had gone on at this camp.

As they prepared to join the rear guard of the column, Eagle Feather and his brothers took a last look at the valley. Yes, it had been a good summer for them.

Suddenly the great buffalo herd below them began to stir. Something was disturbing them. At first the beasts just milled about in confusion then some sectors of the herd began to stampede up towards their part of the valley. The thunder of their approaching hooves made the ground tremble around them.

The brothers wasted no more time looking. Soon they, too, had disappeared into the shelter of the ravine. They soon caught up with the others and spread word of what was happening out in the grasslands they had just vacated.

"It could just be a hunting party going after the herd," Black Wolf said.

Eagle Feather was not so sure. "If it was a small party, they would not be able to stampede so much of the herd. That herd stretches for many buffalo arrows up the valley. There has to be a good many riders out there."

"Even if it is a big Blackfoot war party and they are looking for us, it might take them some time to locate our campsite," Deer Stalker said hopefully.

Eagle Feather pointed at the sky. Above them they could see that dark, threatening clouds had moved in from the west and there was the occasional rumble of distant thunder. "If the rain comes, our enemies will have no trouble seeing our tracks," he said.

Moosekiller fell back from the main column and joined them. He was the only other band member who had a gun. Chief Many Elk had suggested that he do so because he felt that it would be wise to have their most powerful weapons at the rear in case they were pursued. In his view, the guns could break up a charge better than bow and arrows. Firearms were still a novelty in this region and the Chief felt they had a bit of a shock value, causing any pursuer to stop and seek cover.

A light rain had begun to fall and the thunder had moved much closer. The big hound, Kakwa, who had been running alongside quite happily, began to whine uneasily. Like most dogs, Kakwa was terrified of thunder. The rain grew heavier.

"This will make travel much slower for us," Black Wolf observed.

"It will also make the going harder for anyone pursuing us," Moosekiller pointed out.

"You two had better make sure you keep your powder dry," Eagle Feather warned. "A gun that will not fire is of no use to us.'

"I cannot see the Blackfoot following us very far in this weather," Coyote said. "A Blackfoot does not feel very happy fighting in the mountains, I have been told. The rain would only make it worse for them." Coyote had insisted on riding with the rear guard in spite of Crocus' misgivings. If there was going to be trouble, he did not want to miss it.

"That would depend on how determined their leader was," his father pointed out. "I would imagine they would be led by the Sarcee, Lone Eagle. You should know all about him, my son. From what you have told me he would be very determined to get his prize horse back and to capture the ones who stole it."

"I did not steal Silver Runner," Coyote shrugged. "I rode home on my own horse."

The trail had begun a steady rise, so that now they were moving along high above the creek that had been right beside the trail when they had started out. At this point it was possible to look far back over the route they had traveled. The only one who was looking back was Coyote, who had half turned in his saddle while he was talking to his father.

Suddenly he let out a shout. "Look! There are riders back there and a whole lot of them."

The others turned at his cry and looked to where he pointed.

"At this distance it is hard to be sure," Moosekiller nodded, "but I would say about fifty riders."

"And we number about thirty-two at best," Eagle Feather said calmly. "But the odds are not bad for us, because we hold the high ground."

He looked at the trail ahead and was heartened by what he saw. The ravine narrowed considerably at this point. On the one side it dropped off steeply into a narrow canyon far below. Down there the creek was deeper and swifter. On the other side, the mountain rose abruptly and was densely covered with brush and trees.

"I say we should make our stand here," Eagle Feather advised. "At best they could only come at us two at a time, more likely only one at a time."

The others readily agreed. If they made a stand here, the advantage would be in their favor.

"Coyote, I want you to ride ahead and tell the whole column what is happening," Eagle Feather said. "Tell the warriors they are to fall back and join us." Then he remembered that their leader was Chief Many Elk, so he added, "I mean tell the Chief that we want all the warriors back here."

Coyote grinned at his uncle and nodded, then swung away. "Tell the rest to keep going and to move a bit faster if they can," Eagle Feather shouted after him.

The others had dismounted and were waiting for Eagle Feather's instructions. Many Elk had not named Eagle Feather as his war chief, but everyone of the rearguard assumed that he would lead them. They were certain that the Chief would not choose to come back with the warriors. He was an older man and would be more trouble than help to them in battle. The Chief's job was to lead their families away from here to safety and they hoped he would see it that way.

"But what if Many Elk does come back with the warriors?" Black Wolf asked his brother.

"He will not," Eagle Feather said. "He has too much sense to do that."

Pretty soon the whole battle force was assembled around Eagle Feather. Among them was Sun Calf who looked defiantly at his father when the latter gave him a questioning glance, but Eagle Feather did not order him to go back and travel with the families. His son was growing up and having to fight for survival was all part of being a Nakoda. He prayed that the Great Spirit would watch over him.

The rain had become a downpour now – a hard driving force that sent rivulets of water cascading down the steep part of the trail that they had just come over.

Eagle Feather shook his head in disbelief. "I would question the wisdom of any leader who would try to lead a charge up that trail on horseback. I know that is the way the Blackfoot like to fight and the Sarcee, too. That might be the best way to fight out on the open plains, but here in the mountains...?"

The others nodded in agreement, somewhat heartened by his assessment of the situation. There was every indication that they would win this battle, but at what cost none could say.

****

Chapter XIII
The Attack

The first sign of the enemy's approach was a snarl from Kakwa. He stood stiff-legged facing down trail, the hackles rising on his back. Soon a long line of horsemen came into view. All had their lances at the ready.

"I cannot believe it," Moosekiller muttered, shaking his head. "They look like they are all set to charge somebody and they are slogging through heavy mud. They could not even get their horses to gallop in that stuff."

"You were right, father," Coyote said to Deer Stalker. "It is Lone Eagle. I can see him down there. He is the one in charge of this war party."

"Sometimes when a man is full of anger he forsakes all wisdom," Eagle Feather said.

The oncoming warriors were not even aware that the Nakoda were waiting for them above. They moved with caution, all too aware of the slippery trail and the deep canyon, which yawned on their left.

"What should we do?" Black Wolf asked his brother.

"Use your gun. Take out the leader or his horse, if you can," Eagle Feather told him.

Black Wolf raised his gun and pulled the trigger but there was no sound, no belching flame and smoke. "My powder must be wet!" he gasped.

Moosekiller did the job for him and gave a grunt of satisfaction when a rider went down, but it was not Lone Eagle. The shot caught the advancing warriors completely by surprise. For a moment they mulled around in some confusion, hampered by a lack of space in which to maneuver.

"When they move again, as I expect they will, use your hunting bows," Eagle Feather ordered. "I want to see a shower of arrows hit them like a single blow." He was fully in charge now and his men followed his orders without question.

The enemy had drawn back and there seemed to be a lot of arguing going on. One tall figure moved among them. It was Lone Eagle. He appeared to be urging them forward.

"If you get a chance to pick him off, do it," Eagle Feather said to Moosekiller. "I have an idea this whole attack would fall apart if he were gone."

Moosekiller nodded. He had been thinking the same thing and had reloaded his musket with this in mind. "I thought I had a bead on him the first time, but it was someone else I hit."

Suddenly the riders below swept back onto the trail and came charging towards them with lances lowered. The wild battle cry, HIE-YAH-H-H-H, told the Nakoda that there were Blackfoot in this war party, as they had expected.

"They must be crazy," Yellow Bird cried as he released his arrow, quickly plucking another from the quiver behind his back and fired that too. There was a great THWANG as the horde of buffalo arrows sang through the air. By this time Black Wolf had reloaded his gun with dry powder and his shot added to the noise of battle. Moosekiller did not fire this time, he was waiting for his special target.

The charge halted in its tracks. Two or three horses were down and several of the enemy appeared to have been hit, but someone down there also had a gun. A shot rang out below and one of the Nakoda warriors, Red Hawk, let out a cry and went down.

Below them, the Nakoda could see that most of the enemy had abandoned their horses. Those who were still mounted seemed to be urging the others to get back on their mounts and head for home.

"Those would be the Blackfoot," Yellow Bird said. "It is not their fight anyway."

"The more that decide to go home the better for us," Eagle Feather nodded. "But I am wondering what those who are on foot plan to do?"

"I think they are planning to climb up the slope and fire down on us." Black Wolf said.

"I do not like that," Eagle Feather said. "We would soon lose our advantage."

"We can climb up the slope as easily as they can," Deer Stalker pointed out.

Eagle Feather shook his head, "It is true we could do that and we may have to, but it could end all our hopes for an easy victory. We could snipe at one another until nightfall then they could creep among us and engage us hand-to-hand. The advantage would then be theirs because they have more men than we do."

"That is what they are doing," Coyote cried. "They are climbing up the mountain." He had ventured out onto the trail so he could better see what was going on.

"Get back under cover," his father barked. "We have one wounded man; we do not want anymore if we can help it."

"Where is Red Hawk?" Eagle Feather asked.

"Two of his friends carried him back to where the horses are tied and are looking after him," he was told. "The bullet passed through his shoulder. He will be alright."

"We had better start climbing up the mountain," Yellow Bird warned. "We do not want them firing down on us."

Eagle Feather nodded. "We do not have much choice."

Moosekiller was the first to notice that mud was beginning to ooze across the trail from the slope above. He knew from past experience what that meant and reacted quickly. "We have to get out of here!" he shouted, pointing at the ground.

When Eagle Feather saw what was happening he ordered everyone back to where the horses were tethered. Once there, they leapt into their saddles and headed up the trail at a gallop.

"Where is Red Hawk? I do not see him here," Eagle Feather shouted, but his cry was lost in the deep rumble that came from the hillside above. The rumble became a roar as rocks, trees, and bushes came sliding down in a sea of reddish mud, sweeping all before it and burying the trail deeply in a thick layer of debris. On and on came the huge mudslide, pouring over the lip of the canyon and spewing into the stream below.

"The spirit of the mountain is angry," Yellow Bird cried, "and only blood will appease it."

"I wonder how many of our foe was caught in it?" Black Wolf said, as he gazed in awe at the destruction behind them.

"Those who survive will not want to come into our mountains again," Moosekiller said grimly.

"Let us get out of this place," Eagle Feather said wearily. "I am tired of it; if we ride quickly, we might catch up with our families before dark."

Deer Stalker rode up beside him, "You were asking about Red Hawk. I told Sun Calf to find him and help him on his horse and then to get out of here as fast as he could. I did not consult you because you were too busy with the battle."

"You did well brother," Eagle Feather touched him affectionately on the shoulder. "I was worried that he might be caught with us if it came to hand-to-hand fighting. He is young for that sort of thing."

"Some day he will be a great warrior," Deer Stalker smiled. "Sun Calf protested that he did not want to desert you and the others in battle. 'Nakoda warriors do not run from their enemies,' he told me, but in the end he did my bidding."

"I am proud of him," Eagle Feather nodded.

The drenching rain had stopped now and already patches of light were appearing in the overcast sky.

They soon caught up with Sun Calf and Red Hawk. Sun Calf had chosen to ride at an easy pace because he knew that Red Hawk was in pain. When they heard the sound of hoof beats behind them the two had stopped and waited for the others to catch up.

Sun Calf avoided his father's eyes. He still felt a little guilty about leaving the scene of the fighting. Sensing his son's thoughts, Eagle Feather rode up beside him and placed his hand on the boy's shoulder.

"I am proud of you, my son. Today you saved Red Hawk's life."

"I could not have done better myself," Coyote added, who had just joined them.

Sun Calf's spirits rose at this praise. He was anxious to learn how the battle had gone. "Did they leave the field of battle, father? Did they run?" he asked eagerly.

Moosekiller, who was close enough to hear this exchange, let out a bellow of laughter. "No boy, the field of battle left them," he chuckled.

"It left us all," Coyote grinned.

Eagle Feather then explained what had happened. "The whole mountain came sliding down and buried the trail and everyone on it. We had to race for our lives. If you had not put Red Hawk on his horse and moved away from there, he would have been killed. The heavy rain must have loosened the soil."

"The Great Spirit was with us...we lost none," Moosekiller added.

The party dismounted to stretch their legs a bit. Eagle Feather went over to see how Red Hawk was faring. The wounded man's friends had tied a strip of deerskin around the upper part of his arm to stop the wound from bleeding. A wad of soft moss had been placed over the hole where the bullet had left his shoulder.

"The bullet went right through," Red Hawk said with a weak grin.

"And you are still with us," Eagle Feather smiled. "That is the good news. When we get back to Clear Water we will have Otterhead look at your wound. Our medicine Man has many talents."

Eagle Feather gave the order for them to mount up and they obeyed to a man. He had grown in stature among them. They had seen how cool he was in battle and the strategy he had applied against the enemy that had proved so effective. Whether Eagle Feather wanted the job or not, he was their War Chief as far as these warriors were concerned.

Soon they crossed a low divide. The stream that now ran beside the trail was flowing in the same direction that they were traveling. They were certain that this stream had to flow into Clear Water. Then all they would have to do is follow the river home. Their spirits rose.

Coyote, who was riding ahead with his father and two uncles, let out a shout of joy, "I can see the river now."

The trail wound down through a wooded ravine, then burst out into a small meadow where the creek joined Clear Water. Their families were clustered in the meadow and were surrounded by a large group of mounted warriors. For a brief moment Eagle Feather and his warriors paused in dismay, then their faces broke out in smiles and they spurred their mounts forward. The bulky figure astride a white horse in front of them was Otterhead, their Medicine Man.

When the assembled families saw that their men had survived the battle they shouted for joy and rushed to meet them. Everyone started to talk at once in their relief that their men were safe and sound.

A beaming Otterhead rode over to greet Eagle Feather. "When the pack train arrived with the hides and meat, we were told that you might be in trouble," he explained. "They said that you would be coming home this way, so we decided to ride out and meet you."

Chief Many Elk joined them then, all a flutter. "Where is the enemy?" he asked excitedly. "Did you fight them off, or did they just give up the chase?"

Eagle Feather's eyes found Night Star and he smiled at her reassuringly to let her know that all was well.

"We fought them," he told the Chief, as he slid wearily off his horse, "and then the Great Spirit joined the battle."

"And he fought on our side," added Yellow Bird, who was standing nearby.

The rest of the war party had already dismounted and were mingling with their loved ones and the Chief pondered this answer. "Is there any danger that you will be followed?" Many Elk persisted. The Chief was a worrier, much like grandfather, Muskwa.

"No Blackfoot warrior or Sarcee will come here," Eagle Feather assured him. "There is now a mountain between us."

Which was not quite right, but none of them had any way of knowing about the lone figure trudging on foot along the trail they had just traversed.

****

Chapter XIV

A Persistent Foe

When the relief force from the Clear Water camp arrived, Chief Many Elk and his party were resting in this little meadow beside the river, unsure of whether to press on or camp for the night. As soon as Otterhead arrived with his large group of riders, the Chief decided his party should make camp here. Soon darkness would be upon them and he did not relish having to travel an unknown trail at night. No enemy would dare attack them now. When Otterhead and his warriors moved out at dawn to join Eagle Feather and his men at the battle site, the Chief felt he could safely lead the families down river to their base camp. The combined Nakoda force would be too strong for the Blackfoot or Sarcee to overcome them he reasoned.

The Chief had just made this decision and set his people to work, when Eagle Feather and his weary men arrived on the scene. Eagle Feather and his warriors agreed wholeheartedly with this decision. They had been under a lot of tension and now they could relax, have a good meal and later sit around the campfires to tell and retell how they had met the enemy and stopped them in their tracks.

As there were not enough skin teepees in the combined camp for each family to have one, accommodation would have to be shared. Eagle Feather and his two brothers found that there was only a single shelter for their three families. That meant twelve people, including the baby Badger, and the big hound Kakwa. It was a bit of a squeeze for a small traveling teepee, but it was something they had often had to do.

It was sometime before dawn that Coyote was awakened by Kakwa's low growls, Coyote sat up and looked around sleepily. Nobody else was stirring. Then he looked at the dog and found that Kakwa's neck hairs were bristling. Going to the front of the teepee, he opened the flap and stuck his head out. The tethered horses seemed to be uneasy about something. It could be a cougar or a bear he thought. He had better have a look. Grabbing his lance he stepped out of the teepee, closing the flap behind him. He had gone only a short distance when he was suddenly seized from behind and he felt the prick of a knife in the small of his back.

"Where is my horse?" a voice hissed in his ear.

Coyote knew whose voice it was, but he could not reply because the arm around his neck was choking him. He struggled in vain, but the knife only pressed deeper.

Suddenly there was the sound of a heavy blow and the knife fell away. When Coyote swung around, he saw Lone Eagle on the ground groaning and nursing his head. Standing over him was Crocus and Kakwa, both of them in a rage. Crocus was waving a large chunk of firewood and screaming with fury.

By this time, people from the nearby teepees were pouring out to see what all the noise was about.

Coyote went over to Crocus and took the chunk of wood from her. She was now shaking as the reaction set in, so Coyote put an arm around her to calm her down.

"I saw you leave the teepee and I decided to see what you were up to," she panted. "Kakwa came with me. When I saw what was happening, I grabbed the largest piece of wood I could find. I was afraid that he might kill you," she added, "and I was very angry."

Moosekiller arrived in time to hear Crocus' last words and he burst out laughing. "Coyote, you better make sure she never gets angry at you."

Coyote had been thinking much the same thing. Once they were married he would have to watch his step.

Finally, Chief Many Elk arrived to take charge of the situation. "What's going on here?" he demanded.

"This is the Sarcee, Lone Eagle," Coyote told him. "He is looking for his horse, Silver Runner. Perhaps he thinks that Dove is here with us."

In the meantime, Eagle Feather and his brothers had the fallen Lone Eagle up on his feet and had tied his hands behind him. The Sarcee regarded them all with disdain. Did these people, who crowded around him, not know that among the Sarcee he was regarded as a great Chief?

Deer Stalker shook his head sadly. "That son of mine always seems to be around where there is trouble."

"When there is trouble, it is good to have a man of action around, brother," Eagle Feather said. "I would not be too hard on him." Then his face broke into a grin, "And it looks like he is going to have a wife who is ready for action too."

All the people around them laughed at that, including Black Wolf, but he was proud at the way his daughter had rushed to Coyote's rescue.

Eagle Feather looked at Chief Many Elk. "What do you want to do with our prisoner? Do you want to take charge of him?"

"As Chief of the band, I will appoint you and your brothers to take charge of him," he said quickly. Many Elk was no slouch when it came to making that kind of decision.

Eagle Feather looked at Lone Eagle curiously. This was the leader of that mixed band of Sarcee and Blackfoot that had made that foolish attack on their position back on the trail. He did not appear to be a foolish man. Finally he spoke. "Why did you pursue us? We had left the Ya Ha Tinda. The hunting was all yours."

"I want only what is mine," Lone Eagle spat. He pointed a long finger at Coyote. "That young man stole my favorite horse."

"I did not steal Silver Runner," Coyote said angrily. He was still smarting from that knife pointed in his back. "I rode home on my own horse. The woman, Dove, took him so that she could return to her people."

"Where is Silver Runner?" Lone Eagle turned to Eagle Feather, who he sensed was the real leader here. "If you give me my horse, you can keep the woman and I will leave you in peace."

"We were living in peace when you took my nephew prisoner," Eagle Feather pointed out. "Only since that time have we been in turmoil. We do not have your horse or the young woman, Dove. She is well on her way home with a group of Nakoda from Cold Water."

"Can you not see that I could not have taken Silver Runner?" Coyote blurted out. "He would have bucked me off. Dove was the only one he would let ride him, except for you."

Lone Eagle looked crestfallen. At last he could see that Coyote's words made sense. He had been a fool to come here. He looked in amazement at the swelling number of Nakoda warriors gathering around him. "You deceived me," he snarled at Coyote. "You said that yours was only a small party of hunters."

Coyote just shrugged, looking rather pleased with himself. Was it not the duty of a warrior to deceive the enemy if he could?

Chief Many Elk was worried. Dawn was just breaking and a soft mantle of morning mist hung over the river. Soon they must be on their way, but what should be done about their prisoner?

He was the Chief, so the final decision as to Lone Eagle's fate lay with him. To his relief he saw his alter ego, Otterhead, come striding up to the group. Otterhead was a man who liked to linger in his sleeping robes, but he possessed certain wisdom and this situation called for wisdom, much wisdom. He explained his dilemma briefly to the Medicine Man.

"Get the opinion of the crowd," Otterhead advised. "Then if things go wrong you can blame them."

Many Elk's eyes brightened at this suggestion. Of course, why had he not thought of that? He beckoned his people around him and explained. "A decision must be made about our prisoner," he told them. "And it did not take long for me to realize that such a decision must be made by my people. I have great respect for the wisdom of my people."

"We should kill him," Moosekiller spoke from the edge of the crowd. "That would then be the end of it. It would be too much trouble for us to try to keep him a prisoner."

This made sense to most of those assembled and they answered with a shout of agreement. "Kill the Sarcee. If we were their prisoners, they would torture and kill us: that is their way."

The Chief looked uncomfortable. Who would do the killing? "But that is not the Nakoda way," he said finally. He looked at Eagle Feather seeking some sort of guidance.

"I agree," the latter nodded. "It is not our way."

He looked at Lone Eagle. "How did you get here?" he asked. "Where is your horse?"

"I came on foot," the Sarcee replied. "My horse is somewhere under the mountain that fell on us, along with my weapons, except for my knife, which was in my belt."

"How did you escape the slide?" Otterhead asked curiously.

I grabbed a tree branch and pulled myself out of danger," was the reply.

Still feeling the effect of the knife in his back Coyote wished he had lost that too.

Eagle Feather was amazed. "How did you get across the slide?" he asked.

"I was ahead of the others. When I pulled myself out, I was on your side of the slope," Lone Eagle said.

"So you still came on, expecting to ride home on Silver Runner?" said Eagle Feather. He was thankful that only one man got across.

He turned to the group. "As I said before, I agree with the Chief. It is one thing to kill a man in battle, but to kill an unarmed man in cold blood, that is not our way."

Most of the people around him began to nod their heads in agreement. "Eagle Feather is right," someone said. "It is not our way."

"But what will we do with him?" Moosekiller demanded.

At this point Chief Many Elk decided it was time to re-establish his authority. Eagle Feather seemed to be getting a little too popular with the people. There was room for only one politician in the band, well perhaps two. Otterhead was nothing if not a politician.

"Take him back to camp and let the Council decide," Otterhead hissed in his ear.

The Chief cleared his throat. "I have decided that we should take him back to camp and let the Council decide," he boomed, happy that he would not have to make a decision on the spot.

Daylight was upon them now. The mantle of mist along the river was beginning to melt away. After their morning meal everyone began to pack up for the journey home. Lone Eagle was fed along with the rest. Coyote had told his uncle that when he was Long Eagle's prisoner, the latter had seen that he was fed. For the journey down river to their main camp, Lone Eagle did not ride a horse in dignity as befitted a person of his rank. He made the journey lashed to a travois, along with the party's supplies.

Their arrival at the Clear Water encampment was greeted by a great fanfare of barking dogs and shouting children. People rushed out of the lodges waving and calling greetings to those who had been away all summer. The glum-looking prisoner tied to the travois received many curious glances, but there was no open hostility. Everyone was anxious to question the travelers about their journeys and especially how they came to have a prisoner with them. Had there been a great battle?

The big question in Chief Many Elk's mind was how he was going to present the prisoner's case to the Council. Of course, his first task would be to call a Council meeting. As soon as he dismounted, he spread the word around that there would be a meeting that evening.

As might be expected, the Council Lodge was packed with people. Those not able to get in took up various positions outside. This was a big event to them, a break from the monotony of camp life.

With his hands still tied behind him, Lone Eagle was marched inside. The Chief then explained the circumstances surrounding his capture. He did not actually claim to have had a hand in the man's capture, but he chose his words in such a way as to assure his people that he had been on top of the situation right from the start.

Then Eagle Feather was called on to tell how they have been forced to end their hunting in the Ya Ha Tinda and return home by way of the trail through the mountains because of a threat from a combined force of Sarcee and Blackfoot.

This caused quite a stir and the prisoner received some baleful glances, not to mention a few harsh words. He took this with an air of dignity and disdain as befitting a Sarcee Chief.

Next up was Coyote, who told about his capture by Lone Eagle and his party, and how he thus learned of the threat of an attack by superior forces on their Ya Ha Tinda camp. Without taking any glory for himself, he told how he was able to escape the Sarcee camp and bring the warning back to his people. He told how the woman, Dove who was a Nakoda captive of the Sarcee, had freed him from his bonds and ridden back with him on Silver Runner, the prized stallion of their captive, Lone Eagle.

"I told them there would be trouble," Grandfather Muskwa said to those around him when his grandson had finished. Muskwa always managed to find a seat inside the Council Lodge and could always be relied on to voice his opinions.

As the first person to fire a shot in the battle, Moosekiller figured that he was the best one to describe it. The Council had no objections to this so he received the nod. Only the Chief had a few misgivings.

His feelings were justified when Moosekiller launched into what amounted to a hymn of praise for the skilled leadership of Eagle Feather. Everyone gasped in awe as he described the great rain of arrows that struck the oncoming enemy as a single blow, the idea of which had come from the valiant leader, Eagle Feather. When he told of the mighty roar that came from the sliding mountain as it swept their enemies to their deaths in the deep canyon below, the crowd let out a great roar of its own.

"Hoy, Hoy," they shouted in approval.

"The Great Spirit commanded the mountain to move," someone cried. The others took up the chorus, "The Great Spirit won this battle for us."

This was what the Chief wanted to hear. He sprang to his feet and shouted, "It is the Great Spirit we have to thank for this victory." Out of the corner of his eye he noted Otterhead's nod of approval. They did not want Eagle Feather to receive all the acclaim and attention. After all, were they not the official leaders of this band?

Through all this Lone Eagle stood in dignified silence. If he felt any qualms about what his fate might be, he disdained to show it. In the end it was decided that Lone Eagle should be set free to find his way home. With all the meat and hides the band now had to see them through the ravages of Coldmaker, the people were in a generous mood. Let the Sarcee go. Even Red Hawk, whose wound was healing well, felt no animosity towards their prisoner. It had been a good fight and the enemy had lost so much more than they had.

Lone Eagle was offered a choice of remaining captive for the night or leaving right now. Naturally he chose the latter. His request for a bow and some arrows so that he could hunt for game was turned down. They let him keep his knife.

"Give him a supply of pemmican," Eagle Feather suggested. "And some new moccasins," he added, seeing the sorry state of those that Lone Eagle had on.

This was done and the tall Sarcee strode off down towards the river with what dignity he could muster.

Chief Many Elk heaved a sigh of relief that this thorny problem was now behind him.

Next morning, the camp awoke to find one of their horses missing. It had been tethered to a teepee on the edge of the camp and was an easy steal.

"He must have waited a short distance away until we were all sleeping," Eagle Feather laughed, "and then crept back among us." He felt no real animosity towards the Sarcee leader either. He grudgingly admitted that Lone Eagle was a bold and tenacious adversary.

Chief Many Elk, however, could see no humour in the situation. "In four suns he could be back with a large party of warriors to ravage our camp and steal our meat and buffalo hides," he warned.

After consulting with Otterhead and some of the elders, the Chief decided that tomorrow they should leave for their permanent quarters on the big stream called River Boiling. There they would be safe and have lots of time to prepare for Coldmaker. Word was spread through the camp. There were only a few who objected. Most felt that it was time to head for home.

"Many Elk worries like an old woman," Moosekiller said to Eagle Feather.

"It was his worries about an early attack by our enemies when we were in the Ya Ha Tinda that saved us," the latter reminded him. "If we had decided to stay overnight, we would have been lost."

****

Chapter XV

Epilogue

It was their last night at Clear Water. The families of Muskwa and Moraha were in a festive mood. Their summer in the Ya Ha Tinda was one they would long remember. There had been times of stress and times of triumph and the band had acquired a wealth of food and buffalo hides. Tomorrow they would begin the long journey to their permanent home on that grassy plain on the banks of River Boiling that had been named after Old Star, a Kootenai captive who had remained with the Nakoda and later became a Chief among them.

Muskwa and Moraha were glad to be going home. There was a chill on the night air. Back home their lodges were double-walled to keep out the harsh breath of Coldmaker. Far within the big mountains they would be safe from their enemies.

Tonight was a time of gladness – a time to thank the Great Spirit that they had all come through safely. The fire in the teepee of Eagle Feather where they had all gathered lit up their faces, as they relived their summer experiences.

Old Muskwa chuckled, "Long will it be told around the campfires of our people how my grandson, Coyote, was captured and escaped with the Chief's best horse and probably his best woman."

Coyote, who had been sitting quietly with Crocus, looked a bit uncomfortable at this version of the story. Most of the glory belonged to Dove.

"They will sing more songs of how our son Eagle Feather led the Nakoda to victory in battle," old Moraha said.

"And they will forever tell how my Crocus felled a great Sarcee Chief with a piece of firewood," Coyote added, which brought him a warm smile from Crocus.

Keena decided that it was time they paid a bit of attention to the younger family members, "And what about my brother, Wolf Child, who stood up to a charging bear to save Crocus and me?"

Wolf Child looked modestly at the floor until brother, Sun Calf, gave him a friendly poke in the ribs, then his face broke into a grin. "When I slipped and fell, my sister Keena rushed in to save me," he said.

It was at this point that Morning Cloud decided to tell everyone that she was going to have a baby. Deer Stalker was surprised, but delighted at the news. His brother, Black Wolf, slapped him on the back. "You will have another Coyote to hunt with you," he smiled.

"Or another Crocus to brighten our teepee," Morning Cloud reminded him.

Night Star, who had been helping Grey Dawn bathe Badger, laughed out loud. "Men are always seeking an image of themselves."

Then Morning Cloud surprised them again, "I pray the Great Spirit, the Creator, will be with Moraha and me when the times comes for the little one to join us."

Moraha, who had been sadly reflecting that she would have no part in this delivery, broke into a broad smile and came over and hugged her daughter-in-law. Everyone now knew that the cloud that had lain between them was now gone.

"It is good that there will be harmony among us when old Coldmaker holds us trapped in our lodges," Muskwa observed.

Morning Cloud's announcement got Coyote thinking about his black mare. Was she, like his aunt Morning Cloud, also likely to have a little one? If so, that would be his day of reckoning with Lone Eagle, the Sarcee.

As the fire's shadows danced around the teepee's walls, the only other occupant of the lodge seemed completely oblivious to these great events. The hound, Kakwa, could be heard snoring peacefully at the rear of the teepee.

****

GLOSSARY

First Moon of the Golden Eagle................March

Second Moon of the Golden Eagle............ May

The Moon of New Grass........................June

The Moon of Red Berries...................... July

Coldmaker...................................... Winter

Old House...................................... Rocky Mountain House

River Boiling.................................. North Saskatchewan River

Clear Water................................... Clearwater River

Elk River...................................... Red Deer River

Cold Water.................................... Bow River